Folklore: The Second Tale

Chris Rush

Acknowledgements

My thanks firstly goes to you, the reader, for taking
the time to read and support my work.
Thanks to my family and friends for their continued
support.
Thanks to Lisa V. Proulx for editing this story for me.
Thanks to All Things Rotten for creating an awesome
cover.

"I love you so much. Please believe me when I say it wasn't me. Stay out of those fields!" Stephen McKenna.

Prologue

The rain beat relentlessly without mercy against the countryside, as the wind howled its chorus. A trembling light frantically swept through the darkness, from left to right as the desperate calls for Thomas were muted by the ever-growing gales.

Climbing over the heavy, rust ridden gate, a woman and her young son entered the huge, open field.

"Thomas, where are you?" she once again roared, in an effort to find any indication of his whereabouts with the torch.

A farming man, Thomas had become distant lately and very rarely tended to the various chores around the farm or had little interaction with his family, something which was uncharacteristic for him. Susan, his wife found the situation increasingly tormenting due to being the only parent interested in caring for their infant child alongside their son, Sean. Many times she had tried talking to him about what he was going through and the disgruntled man mostly responded with a dismissive "I'm sorry, but you wouldn't understand."

"He has to be out here, I seen him going this way Mammy," Sean said, trying to tuck his head beneath his mother's arm as far as possible to shelter himself from the torrents beating against his face.

"I hope so," she replied, trying not to let the growing worry of her missing husband and infant child overcome her. "Thomas please come back home, everything will be okay I promise," she pleaded, loudly through the thick darkness and harsh elements.

"Mammy look!" The boy shouted moments later squeezing her jacket sleeve tightly.

Turning the light to the direction which the child was pointing towards, Susan eyed a shaking figure in the distance. As they began to slowly step towards it, Susan quickly recognised her husband.

"Thomas!" she called, racing to him with her son close beside her.

Before reaching him, the pair heard his painful wailing, and the closer they got, the louder it became, so much so it drowned out the fierce winds around them.

"What's wrong? Where is our daughter?" Susan asked, watching his shoulders rattle in an up and downward motion due to his immense sobbing.

He didn't answer.

"Thomas?" she asked once again, holding Sean close as she rounded her husband's shoulder.

"They took her from us, they took her," the distraught man sobbed looking down.

Shining the torch downwards she saw him cradling their child in his arms. She then quickly shone the torch around the darkness and eyed an earthen mound in the field, surrounded by a thick ditch, with heavy trees within it in the distance, she then turned the light back to Thomas.

"Come on we need to get her inside before she gets pneumonia," Susan said reaching out and placing a hand on her husband's shoulder.

"She isn't our child, they took her and I couldn't do anything to stop them!" He turned, crying back to his wife.

Looking into his eyes, she could see he believed one hundred percent in every word he spoke.

"Thomas look at her, she will get sick out here," Susan said, "I'll take her," she said holding out her arms, looking down at the rain splashing against the tiny child's face who was wrapped in an old blanket.

Thomas looked at his wife and then to his son standing beside her as the combination of tears and water drenched and ran down along his cold, pale face.

"No it's okay," he finally said, "I'll bring her back in."

He climbed to his feet as Susan ensured the baby was wrapped up as much as possible in the blanket, she then linked his arm, and the family turned to leave the waterlogged terrain towards their home. She did find it unusual that the new born child was not crying due to being exposed to such terrible conditions, however her main concern was to get her back indoors to shelter and warmth as quickly as possible.

"Here let me," she said to her husband, reaching

out her hands to the baby as they stepped into their home.

"I'm so sorry Susan I don't know what got into me and no you're fine I'll put her to bed," he replied quickly, walking away from her towards the infant's bedroom.

Not wanting to cause any more upset, she bit her tongue and allowed him to bring their daughter to bed, while she reassured their son that everything would be okay. Observing closely, she listened as Thomas lay their baby to rest, he then came out of the room and went to their bedroom quickly closing the door behind him without saying another word.

This was the final straw for Susan, she had been pushed to her limits and was determined to get Thomas to go to the doctors the following day. If he didn't agree, she was leaving the house with the children, because there was no way she was going to allow them to be put in danger like that ever again.

Opening the bedroom door and peeking inside, she eyed the small cot and heard the subtle, peaceful breathing inside as the nightlight and soft nursey rhyme played in the background. At least she is warm and asleep now, no point in waking her until she is ready for her feed, she thought to herself while gently shutting over the door once more.

After checking on Sean and ensuring the back and front doors were locked, Susan decided to spend the night on the sitting room couch. Glancing to the clock she saw it was half past one. She was struggling to contain the anger inside her for what Thomas had done but rather than have a full blown war in front of the children, she decided to sort it once and for all the next morning.

Switching off the light she made her way over to her bed for the remainder of the night. Various thoughts wrestled for position in her mind in relation to the recent events however, after an hour or so she finally drifted off to sleep.

The sounds of distant crying awoke Susan from her slumber, checking her phone, the screen clock displayed 05:53. Rubbing her still sleepy eyes she pulled her weary body up to a sitting position on the couch. She turned and spotted the kitchen door ajar with the light on. Susan quickly jumped to her feet hearing her husband's cries grow louder with each passing second.

Pushing open the door, her eyes widened in terror finding Thomas standing at the kitchen table, splattered with blood, holding a large knife.

"Thomas what have you done?" Susan roared, eyeing the cot blankets on the table saturated bright crimson, as a tiny pool of blood began to gather at his feet.

"Thomas?" she shouted once more moving towards the table.

"I couldn't live with it Susan, I am so sorry. I should have protected us but I can't, I can't," he cried, hands shaking.

Looking down at the slashed, bloodied mess on the table before her, the taste of vomit stung the back of her throat.

"I had to Susan, she wasn't our daughter. I should have never went into those fields," Thomas sobbed.

"You're sick! You're going to rot in prison for this, how could you kill your own flesh and blood?" She turned to her husband and began to slap and beat him with rage and tears in her eyes.

He didn't try to defend himself, he replied with, "I love you so much and I'm sorry I let them take our happiness from us. Stay out of those fields!"

Those were his final words before collapsing to the floor holding his face in his rattling, bloodied hands.

Ensuring that she didn't turn her back to the monster on the floor in front of her, Susan slowly stepped backwards into the sitting room, trying her upmost not to look towards the horrific scene laid out on the kitchen table. She reached down, picked up her phone and called the Gardaí, while she turned to see if the sitting room door was still closed, there was no way she wanted her son to witness what his father had done to his sister.

The Gardaí arrived a short time later, each one of the Garda's faces turned ashen and their eyes widened with disgust once they uncovered the true extent of the damage caused by Thomas and the blood soaked blade beside him on the floor. He was arrested instantly and brought to the nearest Garda station.

He refused legal aid and didn't change his story once during the trial, stating that, "They took his child and what he killed was not his daughter."

Thomas was sentenced to life imprisonment, while Susan tried her best to pull herself together for the sake of her son and raise him as best she could.

As Sean grew older, he helped his aging mother around the dying farm to try and keep some form of income coming into the household. He never once visited his father in prison as he grew into a man, nor did Susan and not once did the thought of forgiveness cross their minds for what he did to Sean's sister.

During his incarceration, Thomas quickly became recluse, not interacting with anyone. He would spend the majority of the day and night in his small cell whispering inconceivable wordings to himself. He would occasionally utter brief sentences like "They are real," "Keep my family away from there," and "I didn't kill her," before returning to the random, low, mumbo jumbo.

After a number of years in prison, Thomas developed bowel cancer which quickly impacted his health and appearance. He was offered medical care and managed to send numerous letters to his wife and son, stating his illness and how his last wishes were to see them once more before he died within the cold, thick, concrete walls around him. However, neither Susan nor Sean replied to the letters, each opting to let him suffer and rot for what he had done to the family.

Soon after he sent, what was to be, his final letter, Thomas died roaring in agony, calling for his wife and son with his last breaths.

News was sent to Susan of her husband's death, however she wanted nothing to do with the funeral arrangements and left it entirely to his family. When the day of the funeral arrived, both Susan and Sean stayed as far away as possible, in their minds he died the night he committed the brutal, sickening murder.

Chapter 1

The hypnotising, flickering sunlight was casting its final glow across the dying countryside as the chill began to entomb the land. After living in the city for some time, Stephen McKenna, his wife Louise, and their two children, Owen and John moved to an old Irish cottage in the rural, beautiful Irish countryside.

Stephen followed his dream of owning a house in the country and purchased the cottage which came at a reasonable price due to the various repairs needed on and around the structure. The sale came with a large piece of land which sat adjacent to a huge open field with a silhouette of a small grouping of trees beyond its border. The move was made easier due to Louise's fondness for the countryside and the outdoors. She would often travel from the city and spend hours strolling the hills outside Dublin with friends and sometimes on her own, something which Stephen wasn't too keen on, because if she were to be involved in an accident, phone coverage wasn't great in certain areas and plus she would have no one to help her.

To the left of the cottage stood a much more modern building which was occupied by Mary, a middle aged widowed woman who lived with her eight year old daughter, Claire.

The once vibrant various colours of green splattered throughout the area were beginning to fade and turn to a dull orange or murky brown. Stephen had a passion for restoration and at thirty-five owned a successful building business, so buying the house was the perfect project for him to develop a comfortable family home for his loved ones. With the couple expecting their next child, Stephen suggested they wait until the baby was born until committing to the move, however Louise didn't want to let the pregnancy stop them from securing their dream and promised him she would take it easy.

After glancing at his watch, Stephen called to the children who were playing in the large front garden, "Kids, tea time,"

He had spent the entire Sunday afternoon replacing broken roof tiles on the house, a task which he found tedious because he had to be extremely careful in order not to crack or displace any further tiles while trying to fit the new ones to the roof. He considered retiling the entire roof but that would have immediately contradicted his plan to keep the integrity of the old structure intact and it felt like the easy way out.

"John, Owen, don't make me come down there now," he shouted from the ladder, with a slight grin on his face teasing them, knowing that they knew he was jokingly raising his voice to them.

Smelling the mouth-watering aroma floating from the kitchen window he knew it was time to go inside and wash up for dinner. Turning to take in the last of the daylight losing its grip to the darkness, Stephen deeply inhaled the fresh air and enjoyed the sight of the scenery before him.

He climbed down from the ladder and again called to the children whose playful laugher filled his ears. Owen was six and John had recently turned nine, they both had been close from a young age and both loved to spend time outdoors playing, their parents thankful technology had not taken over.

"Come here you two," The tall father chuckled before giving chase.

Both children squealed with excitement as their father joined in the game. He latched onto and lifting the two of them he said,

"It's harder trying to catch you two than working up there."

Kissing them both on the head, they followed him inside.

Stepping through the sitting room, they eyed Louise in the kitchen scooping mashed potatoes onto four plates, followed by peas, carrots and succulent, and plump pork chops which were then each splashed with a thick gravy. Stephen had instantly fallen in love with Louise's fun personality and sense of humour, which was also helped by her dark brown eyes, long brunette hair, and beautiful spellbinding smile. A smile was something which she was just about managing to display once again following the heartbreak she and Stephen had endured after losing their third child to miscarriage three years previously. It had been a trying time for the couple. Having two young children to look after meant they had little time to comfort each other during their time of grief. Louise instantly blamed herself when the couple received the earth- shattering news in the hospital. She spent many days crying uncontrollably when the boys went to school and when Stephen returned to work, something which he was reluctant to do as he wanted to comfort his wife as much as possible, however that didn't pay the bills.

Once the sale agreement came through, both viewed the move to their new home as a fresh start and a method of helping them move on and dealing with the death of their child. The couple made the decision to try once more for a third child sometime afterwards and Louise revealed the news to her husband she was pregnant two months before moving into their new home.

"Looks amazing," Stephen said, leaning over to Louise and giving her a kiss on her soft cheek.

"Thank you, you had good timing," she smiled.

"You said five O' clock and I could tell by the smell it was ready, plus I'm starving," he chuckled.

"Okay you little rascals, go wash those hands before you eat. That means you too," she said turning back to her husband.

After the meal, the family spent the evening watching television together. The children enjoyed watching the family gameshows and happily sat on the floor in front of the television until they were called to brush their teeth for bed.

"Can't believe we've been here a month and we still haven't talked properly to one of our new neighbours. We only know Mary next door from bumping into her from time to time when she is out in the garden, but she seems really nice," Louise joked while undressing for bed later that night. Stephen was thrilled to see his wife returning to her former self after their tragic loss.

"Well it's not as if it's a buzzing city we are living in or anything," Stephen sniggered. "Yeah Mary is lovely. The closest thing to us other than Mary and her daughter is the farm up the road and after that it's probably at least a five minute drive from here to the next house, you want to do a door to door introduction?" He asked turning to her unable to hide the huge smile cracking across his face.

"Very funny aren't you?" Louise replied, walking over to him and gave him a playful slap on the shoulder. "I love this place so much, but I love you even more," she said, wrapping her arms around him and kissing him softly.

"It's perfect here isn't it? Won't be long until we have a new little member to the family," he smiled, rubbing Louise's stomach.

"I know," Louise said smiling, feeling nervous, due to the previous pregnancy.

"Let's hope I get this place sorted first before he or she arrives," Stephen said, knowing there was a lot work ahead of them in order to get the old cottage up to the vision they both had for it.

"Don't worry. It's perfect and I'm sure you will," Louise said hugging her husband tightly thinking of the life they were going to share together in their new home.

"I've noticed Mary has quite a few male friends," Louise continued as she moved back over towards the bed.

"What do you mean?" asked her husband.

"Well when her daughter is in school, she has quite a lot of visitors who stay a while and leave. Some days more than others."

"I don't even want to think about what you are hinting at. That's an image I don't want in my head," Stephen laughed, "Maybe they are just friends eh?"

"Yeah maybe," Louise smiled, noting his sarcasm.

"Come on time to get up," Stephen called to the children the following, overcast Monday morning.

This was the usual routine on school mornings as Louise prepared breakfast for the family. Living quite a distance from the nearest village meant the children had to get up very early, eat their breakfast, and get ready for school before the bus collected them at approximately 8:20 each morning.

"You working late this evening?" Louise asked, pouring Stephen a cup of tea.

"Yeah I think so, the buyers want to move into the house as soon as possible. So, the quicker I get finished, the faster we get the final payment," he said sipping the hot beverage.

"No problem, I'll keep dinner hot for you."

He smiled in appreciation.

"Morning sleepy heads," Louise said, turning to the brothers walking into the kitchen.

Looking at his sons sitting at the table in front of him, Stephen remembered the words his parents had said to him so many times during his childhood. "Your school days are the best days of your life." He turned his attention towards his hands, which had been victims of many a cut and bruising due to years of manual labour, knowing those very words had turned out to be true, however he wouldn't change his ways because he believed in working hard to achieve his goals and providing for his loved ones.

"Okay go put on your uniforms," Louise said, collecting their empty bowls and placing them into the warm water within the sink.

The children did as they were told and left the room.

"I'm hoping to finish the last of the broken pieces on the roof this week," Stephen said, finishing his cup of tea.

"Okay well don't go up there in the dark okay? I'm sure some cracked tiles can wait until the weekend," his wife responded knowing he was eager to get the job done and move onto the next.

"I won't, don't worry."

Moments later, Owen and John returned to the

kitchen with their full school attire upon them.

"Okay give Mammy a kiss before going out with Dad," Louise instructed them before they left to wait for the school bus outside as Stephen set off towards work.

Both the children kissed their mother on the cheek and collected their coats at the front door.

"Speak soon okay," Stephen said to Louise before giving her a peck on the lips.

Stepping outside, they were greeted by the overwhelmingly fresh country air. The children were instructed to always wait for the bus to come to a complete stop beyond the old, small, black steel garden gate when it arrived and of course if it was raining they would wait for the recognisable, heavy bus engine sound to make its way along the road before going out into the elements. However that morning there was a stranger leaning against one of the granite gate pillars.

"Morning," the man said with a huge smile etched from cheek to cheek.

"Yeah good morning how are you?" Stephen replied, making sure the children's jackets were zipped up sufficiently to keep them warm.

"You're new here right?" The elderly individual asked adding, "I live in the farmhouse just up the road from here."

"Yeah we are from the city and moved in about a month ago now, still trying to get used to the place," Stephen smiled.

"Yeah I can imagine, it's bound to take some getting used to out here," the man said.

"So what can I do for you?" Stephen asked, stepping towards the man using their gate for support.

"Oh sorry where are my manners. Sean Byrne, nice to meet you," he said introducing himself with an outstretched hand.

"Stephen, nice to meet you too," he smiled, taking Sean's hand in his, instantly noticing the years of wear and tear and embedded dirt in the skin, outlining years of hard work.

"So you live near here?" Stephen continued, as the gentle breeze encouraged the naked trees on the opposite side of the road to sway slightly.

"Yes, I own a small farm and some land around here. Well when I say farm I mean it used to be. I got to the age where I couldn't be chasing cattle around fields anymore and those early mornings would kill you," he chuckled. "Now I just tend to the land as needed with some seasonal help and sell any crops and so forth I can manage to harvest. It's kind of a semi-retirement role," Sean grinned.

"I feel like retiring myself sometimes," Stephen laughed in response.

"Not at all, you've plenty of years ahead of you yet. So I see you moved into the old O' Brien's home, they were a lovely family."

"Yeah, it still needs some more work but we are getting there. Did you know the family? The estate agent didn't tell us much about them," Stephen said turning to check that the children were okay.

"Yes I did, but they kept to themselves and I suppose when their son died, they needed a fresh start."

"Died?" Stephen asked quickly, turning back to his newly discovered neighbour.

"Yeah, such a sad story and at such a young age too. But let's not dwell on that eh, so what's next with the place?" The old farmer asked, changing the subject due to the children being close by.

"I've a bit left on the roof and then going to move onto the inside, a few things need to be replaced."

"Well if you need a hand, I'm happy to help," Turning his attention to the children, Sean continued, "How are you both doing?" He smiled.

Both children pleasantly said hello in return.

"Daddy ask him what that is," John said referring to the structure on the piece of land in the distance.

"Oh I wouldn't go near there, it's dangerous," Sean instructed as he pointed his old, crumpled finger towards what looked like a mound with some trees within it in the distance.

"Dangerous?" Stephen asked, eyes brows scrunched.

"Yes the ground around there isn't great, lots of holes and pits where you could easily snap an ankle, plus due to the layout of the land, the soil is always wet, bad drainage I suppose, so it's very soggy and slippery," he smiled to the children. "But please stay away from there, I don't want any injuries on my land," Sean finished, turning to Stephen with an authoritative tone.

"No problem and thank you for the advice, the little guys were only wondering last week what that was, I was too if I'm being honest," Stephen replied.

Sean dwelled no more on the item on his land and finished with, "Anyway, I better leave you to it. But remember please stay away from there."

"Was nice meeting you Sean," Stephen said with an outstretched hand.

"Yeah, you too," Sean replied, taking him up on the friendly gesture before turning and slowly making his way back up the narrow, country road towards home.

"Stephen?" Came Louise's voice from the front door.

Turning, he walked over to her, patting the children on their heads as he walked by.

"Who was that love?" She asked, watching Sean step towards his house.

"That's Sean, one of our new neighbours," he said.

"Ah it's nice to finally start meeting more people around here isn't it?" Louise replied.

"Yeah he owns the farm and some land around here," Stephen added.

"Really, he still runs a farm at his age?" Louise asked in awe after witnessing the elderly, plump man lumber his way from their gate.

"No, no, from what I could tell he literally just

lives on it now and tends to the land as necessary. He mentioned that mound you said seems out of place across the fields too."

"Oh really, what did he say? Wife? Children? Grandchildren?" Louise asked in return.

"Just that it's dangerous because of the ground up there or something and I'm not sure about him having any family, but he seems really nice."

"Ah that's good, okay, the bus is coming," Louise said to the children hearing the engine chugging in the distance. "Oh hi Mary," she said spotting Mary seeing her daughter off to school.

Stephen and Louise were thankful their children had someone their own age to tag along with on the journey into town on the bus.

"Hi Louise, Stephen," she smiled in return.

"Hello," Stephen waved, turning back, "I better get going too," he said before leaving for work.

Louise kissed Owen and John goodbye before they got onto the bus, closed the door behind her and went back into the kitchen to finish cleaning up after breakfast.

Looking out across the beautiful landscape, she thought of how there were no eye pleasing sights like the one she was currently feasting on in Dublin. Sure in her opinion the city had its beautiful areas, but nothing like this. Her eyes then turned to the earthen mound at the far side of one of the fields in the distance.

After finishing some of the bits and bobs she had

to do around the house, she decided to go over to Mary's to properly get to know the woman she had been living beside over the last month or so.

Reaching into the cupboard, Louise fetched a packet of biscuits and left her house towards Mary's. Louise had been so busy cleaning up around the place, this was her first opportunity to visit their closest neighbour for a chat.

Knocking on the front door, Louise stood and admired the garden which surrounded the house. Mary was a keen gardener and would spend a lot of time ensuring the upkeep of the garden was maintained. When the door opened, Louise was greeted with wide eyes and a huge smile.

"Louise how are you?" Mary asked, her expression making it clear she was happy to see her.

"I'm doing good thanks, I said I would finally call round to say hello properly as I've got the place looking somewhat like a home over there," Louise laughed.

"It's great to see you, come on in," Mary replied.

Mary was a thin woman whose hair was beginning to turn grey. But from what Louise could tell, she seemed to be a gentle soul.

"Have a seat, I'll put the kettle on," Mary said, turning towards the sink to fill it with water.

"I'm sorry I couldn't get around to this sooner, you must have thought we were so ignorant not calling over," Louise said, resting herself on the cushion beneath her.

"Not at all. I know what it's like to move into a new home, it takes a while to settle in and just when you think you're finished with the move, something else pops its head up and has to be taken care of," Mary replied, flicking on the switch.

"You're not wrong there," Louise laughed, "I didn't think I owned as much stuff before I decided to pack and then unpack it."

"I hear you, I remember my parents were the same when we moved here. There were brown boxes everywhere for a few weeks, I don't even know where they found space for it all," Mary said, running her fingers through her hair as she waited for the kettle to boil.

"So you've lived here a while?" Louise asked.

"Yes. I've lived here most of my life. As you can imagine I had Claire at a very late age, her father and I had been trying for a child for so long and we had actually given up hope when she came along to surprise us," Mary replied as she began to prepare two cups of tea.

Her reply brought warmness to Louise's heart hearing that the couple had finally gotten the gift they had been trying so hard to obtain.

"That's so nice to hear, I bet she is spoilt rotten," Louise responded taking the warm cup of tea in her hand from Mary.

"Oh, you can bet on that, she was the apple of her father's eye," Mary said, leaving the sugar and milk in front of Louise and then she sat down opposite her.

"Was?"

"Unfortunately my husband only got to enjoy two of Claire's birthdays before he passed away," Mary replied with a faraway look in her eyes.

"I'm so sorry. I didn't mean to bring up any hurtful memories," Louise returned, hoping the ground would open up and swallow her whole for probing the woman about why she had used her husband in the past sense.

"Ah no need to be dear, you weren't to know. It was tough I'll admit, but our little angel helped me get through the pain of losing him somewhat. So what made you move here?" Mary asked, taking a sip of the warm tea.

Thankful she hadn't dug her way into a hole, Louise too enjoyed another mouthful of tea and said, "There was too much hustle and bustle in Dublin and to be honest, the cottage was an absolute bargain. Stephen and I have always loved the countryside so this seemed like the perfect choice and I have to admit it is. The place needs a few bits done to it but we're getting there."

"Well it's nice to have someone living in there again and it's so handy that Stephen is a builder too, that will help save some money," Mary replied.

"It really is, he is treating it like his little private project," Louise giggled. "We were told very little about the previous family who lived there, not even why they decided to sell."

Mary paused while taking another mouthful of tea

and stared across the table towards her new neighbour.

"Did the estate agent not say anything at all about them?" Mary asked, and then placed the cup slowly back onto the table.

"No, only they decided to leave after a tragedy. Please tell me no one died in the house?" Louise asked, shivers beginning to make their way through her at the thought.

"No, no dear, no one died in the house," Mary quickly said in an effort to calm Louise. "However, their son went missing and wasn't found until a number of days afterwards, sadly he died from malnutrition."

"Oh my God, where did they find him?" Louise asked in shock.

"They found him out there in the fields. Poor boy lay there in the long grass in torrential rain for quite some time."

"That's terrible, do they know what happened to him?" Louise continued.

"No, his parents had apparently been fighting and he ran away. It was concluded he got lost in the field the night he left home, fell, knocked himself unconscious, and then died out there," Mary explained.

"Poor thing," Louise said raising the cup again, knowing all too well what it was like to lose a child. "Listen, I have to ask, what is that thing at the far side of the fields?"

Again Mary paused, eyes wider this time.

"Oh that?" Mary stuttered, "That is what we old folk call a rath or ring fort. Well at least that's what I think it is, I've never been up there myself."

"A ring fort?" Louise said in a high pitched tone, outlining she hadn't heard the phrase too often before.

"Yeah some have survived from the olden days around the country. They are remnants of days long past however very important to our history. But that one is dangerous, you do better to keep well away," Mary said in a firm tone.

"Yes Sean already told us," Louise replied, wondering how Mary knew it was dangerous if she hadn't been up to it.

"Sean is a lovely man isn't he? But he is right, that place is full of nooks and crannies and very slippery, many people have injured themselves up there," Mary explained.

"It looks so out of place there," Louise stated.

"I agree but who are we to judge where our ancestors built their structures eh?"

"That's true," Louise said in agreement.

The pair spent about an hour longer getting to know each other before Louise had to say farewell.

When Louise returned home, her interest in the rath had increased even further. Being an outdoorsy person, she had wanted to investigate the area for a number of weeks since they moved in, however she thought it best to stay away as instructed.

Later, Stephen and Louise spent the night together watching television once the children had gone to bed.

"Went over to talk properly with Mary today," Louise said, cuddling further into her husband.

"Oh yeah? You did right. She seems like a really nice person," Stephen replied, putting his arm around the love of his life.

"Yes she really is. She told me her husband passed away six years ago."

"Ah no you're joking? What happened?" Stephen asked.

"I didn't want to ask her, I felt so bad she had to explain it to me after I questioned her on why she said her daughter used to be the apple of her father's eye," Louise explained.

"Ah, how were you to know, I'm sure she saw it that way too."

"She did. Listen, she told me the previous owner's son died out in the fields, they had been arguing and he ran away. They didn't find him until a few days later," Louise said, sitting up on the large, soft couch.

"Yeah, Sean told me their son had died when we spoke this morning. But it's nothing to worry about, you okay?" Stephen added, turning to his wife to reassure her.

"He ran away after his parents had an argument. Poor family, I don't blame them for moving away. All those memories," Louise said. "No wonder we got the place so cheap and there was so much to do to it.

I bet they just wanted to get out of here as soon as they could. I can imagine how they must have felt and still feel."

"Yeah makes you appreciate what you have doesn't it?" Stephen said squeezing Louise with a huge hug, to help take her mind off their own loss.

"That's for sure, oh you know what that thing is out there in the fields? She told me it's an old ring fort."

"Oh yeah? Sounds cool, but we better stay away as Sean asked," Stephen quickly added.

"Mary said the same, that it is a dangerous place and to stay away. I guess all the beatings it's gotten over the decades from the weather have taken their toll on it," she replied, resting her head back onto her husband's shoulder.

The couple spent the reminder of the night enjoying their favourite programs before deciding to call it a night.

While Stephen checked on the doors, Louise went to the kitchen to ensure the windows were locked.

Pulling the curtain aside, she checked the cold handle as she stared out into the blackness beyond the glass. Louise couldn't get the thought of the young boy laying out in those dark fields, dead for days out of her mind. She thought of the unimaginable pain and loss the family must of felt when his cold body was found in the grass, and the torment that must have bombarded them knowing it was because of the argument they had which drove him to run away.

Turning, Louise finished checking around the house with Stephen and they retired to bed, both thankful for the lives and happiness they had.

Chapter 2

The following morning came bright, however the countryside had been rinsed in a light drizzle overnight.

The family enjoyed breakfast together before Stephen had to climb into his van to set off to work and the children go to school.

All morning while she was preparing breakfast for the family, Louise occasionally glanced towards the ring fort in the distance. It looked exceptionally mystifying as the early morning mist swayed around it as the sun slowly burnt it away. There was something about the structure which drew Louise's attention to it, almost like a magnet or like someone clicking their fingers once again to turn her concentration back towards it when she tried to focus on something else. Being a lover of the outdoors meant she had visited a lot of sites, however she had never seen anything quite like this on her travels.

Once finished the washing up, Louise carried out some hoovering around the house while watching the sunlight grow brighter outside. However, that landmark in the distance still caught her eye as she occasionally came and went from the kitchen.

It was early afternoon when she finally gave into temptation and decided she would venture up to see what the mysterious, out of place landmark was like in person. Conscious of her current condition, she knew she would have to take strict care and thought that surely Sean would understand her interest in the site as a reason for being on his land if she got caught.

Pulling on her Wellingtons, she stepped out into the sunshine which was accompanied with a cool country air pushing gently past her as she locked the old cottage door behind her. Louise made her way out onto the quiet country road. The peacefulness was another reason Louise and Stephen loved the location. She turned right and stepped towards the old field gate a short walk from their house. She placed her fingers on top of the cold steel with one hand and unlatched it with the other.

Moving through the thick, damp grass, cheered along by the pleasant chirps of the birds dancing above her, Louise's sense of adventure grew with every passing moment. She wondered to herself what indeed lurked behind the mysterious trees and undergrowth on the developing mound in the distance, as she stepped closer and closer.

It's like it just grew there to make itself known. What's in there? She said to herself as she negotiated her way around the small gatherings of surface water along her route.

Following another five minute trek, her house now a tiny feature in the background, Louise reached her unusual destination.

She instantly noticed the aggressively thick

shrubbery, mixed with various branches pointing their way in all directions, the thin branches which reminded her of old, broken, disfigured, arthritic fingers reaching out as if they were trying to take her hand. What baffled her mind more so were the trees. From what she could identify, the earthen mound slowly raised to approximately four feet off the field surface. Looking through the undergrowth she was amazed to see the trunks of the majority of the trees were twisted around one another like uneven coils and the others which stood alone seemed to be warped and bent into various odd shapes and arches.

Moving around the perimeter, Louise guessed the diameter of the unusual piece of earth had to be at least thirty meters in length and the trees themselves contorted their way abnormally high towards the sky.

There was something about this place which seemed to hold her attention effortlessly as she moved about the outside of the mound, as if hypnotising her as she walked its boundary. She could not help but stare hard into the baffling countryside sculpture in front of her. It was then something triggered her attention from the corner of her eye.

Turning, she noticed the beautiful choir which had accompanied her on her way to this bizarre destination had stopped its harmonic tune and an eerie silence befell the land. Trying to adjust her footing on the soft ground for a better view, for a moment Louise thought she could see a small figure with extremely long, dark hair peering from behind one of the thick tree trunks in the centre of the ominous landmark towards her.

"Hello?" she called, the coldness of the countryside becoming more noticeable around her with each passing second.

No reply came from the motionless, unsettling stranger staring back at her.

Without any warning, the snapping of twigs and sounds of rustling quickly drew her eyes to the right, however nothing could be seen, turning back, the illusive spectator had vanished and it was then she began to hear subtle whisperings, "Leave this place, we don't want your kind here, go or you will be ours forever." The words seemed to float beyond the dense ditch boundary before her, followed by the sounds of a crying baby.

Feeling disorientated, she closed her eyes for a moment, trying to rationalise what was happening. In an instant, all was quiet, and all was normal, once more. Opening her eyes, she quickly glanced around the area and nothing other than the strange environmental architecture before her was noticed and the natural countryside sounds had returned.

"Don't be silly, it's all in your head Louise," she rationalised, still feeling a little uneasy on her feet. "I knew I should have had something for lunch earlier."

Wanting to investigate further, she quickly remembered the warning given to the family about the place and the current situation of the soft ground beneath her, she assumed it must be worse beyond the initial border. This combined with her dubious feeling and the fact she was pregnant, Louise decided to call it a day and return home.

Walking back down the field towards safety, Louise couldn't help but turn back and glance at the mound behind her every couple of steps. A sense of being watched crashed over her but she tried to convince herself that she was just being silly.

Unlocking the front door to the small cottage and stepping inside, Louise was shocked to find the clock on the wall read 3:10pm.

"There is no way I was out there for three hours," she said, walking into the sitting room. Turning towards the clock on the old fire mantelpiece, it too read 3:10pm. This was then confounded by checking her mobile phone which turned from 15:10 to 15:11 before her eyes. It was only a little after twelve when I left the house, she thought to herself.

Realising the children would be home from school soon, Louise had to quickly push her bewilderment aside and begin preparing dinner for the family, of which due to her recent time lapse, she was somewhat behind on the preparation.

"Mammy," followed by giddy laughter, came from the front door as Owen and John let themselves in soon afterwards.

Louise had been so caught up in the strangeness of her afternoon, that she didn't hear the heavy groan of the bus's engine outside dropping the children home after school.

Meeting them in the sitting room, she helped each child remove their jacket and then switched on the television to hold their attention while she continued to work on the meal in the kitchen.

It was after five when Stephen returned home from work later that evening. Stepping through the back door, which was at the side of the kitchen extension that had been added to the old cottage before they moved in, he greeted Louise with a kiss and sat at the table with John and Owen, who had left the sitting room and began going through their homework.

"So how was school today?" Stephen asked the children, who each smiled back in return. "Dinner smells lovely honey," he continued turning to Louise who was peeling the potatoes at the sink. The chicken she had taken out of the freezer earlier that morning, was placed into the oven late due to her trip to the mysterious lump of earth in the field, so in turn, dinner was going to be dished up later than usual.

Louise didn't acknowledge his comment. She kept peeling and staring out into the darkness towards the location where she had her unnerving experience earlier that day. The more she thought about it, the more her mind raced for an explanation. She wondered if she really did see the strange figure staring back at her through the thick undergrowth or was it just her mind playing tricks on her, and how did she spend three hours unnoticed out there?

After finishing dinner, Stephen helped Louise

clean up as the children finished their homework in the comfort of the sitting room as the old fireplace emitted a warm, glowing heat about the room. Once the washing up was complete, the pair joined the children and spent the remainder of the evening enjoying each other's company in front of the television. Stephen enjoyed nothing more than relaxing with his loved ones after a hard day's work.

Once bedtime came, John and Owen were sent to brush their teeth and then to bed, during which the volume on the television had to be lowered to allow them to drift off to sleep. Although small and cosy, the old Irish cottage's design meant sound in the sitting room could be easily heard in the bedrooms. Not long after the children were put to bed, the couple decided to call it a day also.

"Is everything okay?" Stephen asked Louise as he got undressed at the foot of the bed.

"Yeah, why do you ask?" Louise replied from beneath the duvet as her long, dark hair draped its way down the side of the mattress.

"I don't know, you just don't seem yourself this evening," her husband said.

The truth was she hadn't felt the same since her strange experience that day and she hadn't had the time to rationalise what she had gone through. She didn't want to feel silly and tried to cover her embarrassment by continuing through the day as normally as possible.

"No, I'm fine thanks, just been a long day," she

said, as she turned and smiled towards him.

"I know that feeling," Stephen grinned.

Switching off the bedroom light, he joined her in the bed and placed his arm firmly around her. Within minutes, he was sound asleep however Louise wasn't so lucky. Her mind kept tormenting her for an answer and finally after battling for about an hour, she managed to close her eyes.

Chapter 3

The next day brought with it an overcast and damp countryside. The events of the day before continued to plague Louise's thoughts and she decided the only way she would be able to ease her mind was to visit the site once again to look for any clues to help explain what had happened. She knew if what had occurred the day before were to happen again, then it would be a cause for alarm, however she was confident she would be kicking herself for overthinking.

Throughout the morning she had, as before, occasionally glanced towards the ominous site in the distance, which was surrounded in a thick, swaying fog, something which seemed to be always present at some stage throughout the day. There was something about the place which kept bringing her attention back to it. It was as though she couldn't think of anything else but that piece of earth watching over their home from a distance.

Stephen had commented on her not being herself that morning however, she again told him she was fine. Once the children had gone to school and Stephen was at work, Louise quickly put on a rain jacket and Wellingtons. Before locking the front door behind her, she looked towards the clock and then her phone, each reading 10:27. She needed to establish the time which she was leaving the house for sure, because there was no way she was going to lose track of a large chunk of time two days in a row for seemingly no reason. Louise felt a little stupid for worrying over the lost three hours, realising she clearly must have misinterpreted the correct time when she left the house the day before and also felt silly for obsessing about a random piece of earth in the middle of a field. However the one thing she wanted to clarify more so was that there had been no one up there with her the day before. She rationalised that her mind had been playing tricks on her however she wanted to be sure.

Looking towards Mary's house as she made her way down the driveway towards the road, it seemed peaceful. Thankful as she didn't want to engage in conversation at that moment, Louise turned and ventured up the road once again. Opening the gate, she made her way toward the cause of her bafflement over the last number of hours. The countryside, although still damp, was extremely serene. One thing she had always noticed while living in Dublin was the continuous sounds of the traffic whizzing by in the distance no matter the time of day or night. Now she enjoyed the peace and quiet and the natural environmental sounds around her, with only the occasional vehicle engine breaking through the relaxing atmosphere.

Nearing the mound, she found it strange the thick

fog seemed to barely breach the perimeter of the circular feature and once it did, it quickly returned inside the ditch, as if it was summoned to do so. Everywhere else around her was clear for quite a distance until the hazy rain obscured her vision.

When she was several steps from the earthen mound, Louise stopped to take in the atmosphere. She checked her phone and noted fifteen minutes had passed. Seems about right, she said to herself as she placed it back into her jacket pocket. Louise waited and nothing seemed to be out of place except for the dancing blanket of fog before her. Stooping, she tried to peer through it however it was no use, Louise couldn't see anything but a thick whiteness and the occasional tree silhouette before it was swallowed by the fog once more. Stepping forward, she decided to make her way inside to see what lurked behind the dense ditch in front of her.

As she got closer, the earth seemed to stand still as the silence grew heavy around her, but she couldn't stop herself from progressing. Louise had to see what hid behind the thick undergrowth before her and experience what it was like amongst the trees which seemed to grow around each other in unnatural ways. Just before pushing her way past one of the heavy bushes, a voice called to her, "Great day for it isn't it?"

Turning, Louise eyed their old farming neighbour Sean, making his way towards her.

"How are you?" She smiled towards him,

wondering what way he was going to react with her being on his land.

"I'm fine thanks. I hope you weren't thinking about going in there, now were you? I told your husband no one must go in there!" he replied. His tone friendly at first, but soon turned firm.

"Why, what's in there?" Louise asked, having never seen anything quite like it in all her years of hiking.

"It's dangerous, that's all you need to know," the farmer replied stepping closer to her.

A few awkward moments of deafening silence fell between the pair and Sean continued by saying, "It's been there for as long as anyone around here can remember. You could easily break a leg in there and if that happened, you could be here for a while being so far from the road and your house."

"I'm sorry I didn't mean to-"

"Not at all, no need to be sorry. I was just out for a stroll myself, even though the weather isn't great, I like getting out for some fresh air to help loosen up these old joints. Anyway, I saw you making your way up through the field so I decided to get to you before you injured yourself."

"You sound like a man speaking from past experiences," Louise said, wondering if he was going to share stories of accidents that had occurred there.

"When my father used to farm this land, he always told me to say out of there. A lot of small holes and crevices, you see, easy to snap an ankle," Sean explained in the same way he had told her husband.

"Ah I see, well thanks for the warning. I was here yesterday and saw the trees inside. Stunningly beautiful," Louise replied.

"You didn't go in did you?" Sean quickly shot back, marching closer to her.

"No… I just looked that's all," the woman answered, uneasiness creeping over her.

Sean's stern expression eased a little, eyebrows returning to a natural position, and his stare became less intense.

"Good, I don't want anyone injuring themselves that's all." Taking a few breaths, he continued, "Listen I'm sorry, I don't mean to come across as a grumpy old so and so, I would just feel terrible if you fell or hurt yourself in there."

"No need to apologise I completely understand," Louise said, thankful he wasn't angry finding her trespassing on his land. "What is it anyway?" she asked.

"To be honest, I don't know but it's been there a long time and treated as a local landmark. Some call it a ring fort, but I have no name for it," Sean explained.

"It reminds me of the remains of an old woods, it just looks so out of place here," Louise said, turning back to the unusual site beside her.

"Yes, it does, doesn't it? It's hard to say really, but either way it's there and it's not safe to go inside, the ground is uneven and extremely slippery. Could be due to all the rain we get around here and when the sun does decide to join us from time to time, its light can't penetrate the treeline," Sean said, smiling towards Louise.

Embarrassed for almost overstepping the farmer's off limits location, she smiled back towards him saying, "Wow I didn't even think of that."

"Okay, best get you away from here. So, you like going for walks?" Sean said, turning from the mound and strolling away for Louise to follow him.

"Yeah I love getting out and about," she said, accompanying him towards the field entrance.

"Well you'll definitely like it around here. Loads of public areas to walk about but just make sure you don't go in there okay?"

"Have you lived here all your life?" Louise asked, taking the subtle hint to stay off his land.

"Yes, and so too did my father and his father. The Byrne's have been around and farmed these parts for quite some time," he smiled.

"That's really nice. Are you married, do you have any children or brothers or sisters?" Louise continued, enjoying getting to know the man as they made their way back towards the gate.

A silence fell between the pair which in turn caused Louise to look towards Sean who by then was staring towards the soggy ground beneath them as they progressed through the grass. Watching his eyes, she couldn't help but sense a sadness swelling within them.

"Sean?" she asked, to ensure he was okay and that

she hadn't overstepped the line.

A few more moments dragged passed until he finally said, "No I'm not married and no children. I used to have a sister but she is gone now," he said, as the memories of how his father had brutally murdered her in the kitchen of the house he still lived in flooded into his mind, however he wasn't going to divulge all the graphic details to Louise.

"Gone?" Louise asked, slightly confused.

"She passed away when I was a young boy," Sean continued.

Instantly upon hearing the statement, Louise wanted to disappear from existence. She couldn't believe she had put her foot in it again with one of her neighbours, like she had done with Mary. She couldn't take the original hint when Sean stated she was gone when referring to his sister.

"Oh my God Sean I'm so sorry! I didn't mean to upset you," Louise replied, looking at his face straining to hold back the emotion.

"It's okay Louise, how were you to know? So, there is no need to apologise okay?"

Louise smiled in return and spoke no more until they reached the gate because she didn't want to add any further awkwardness to the current situation.

"It was nice meeting you Sean," Louise said to him while he opened the gate for her.

"Yeah likewise, if you or Stephen ever need anything just let me know. I only live five minutes away and it's always good to see people."

"Of course, and thank you, feel free to call into us anytime you want okay?" Louise replied.

"I will, thanks. Remember don't go in there." Sean's final words lingered in the chilly air as he turned and began his journey home.

"I met your friend today," Louise said to Stephen later that evening as he sat down to watch a match on television.

"Who is that?" He asked.

"Sean."

"Oh yeah? He is a nice fella isn't he, where did you see him?"

Not wanting to reveal why she had originally gone into the field she answered with, "I met him while I was outside earlier. Yeah, he seems nice but really doesn't want anyone walking around that mound up there, he warned us to stay away from it again today."

"I'm sure he just doesn't want anyone getting hurt. What else did you talk about?" Stephen asked, not taking his eyes off the game.

"Well, I found out he has no wife or children and his only sister died when he was young," Louise replied, cuddling up beside her husband and looking towards a screen she had no interest in viewing.

"What happened to her?" Stephen asked.

"Come on now I couldn't ask him that," she replied.

"Why not?" Stephen grinned.

"Shut up you," she smiled, realising he was teasing

her.

Meanwhile Sean sat beside the open fire taking in its welcome, warming glow. He had a glass of whiskey in hand, something he enjoyed doing occasionally once darkness descended around his property.

Taking a sip of the beverage, he turned his attention to the room beyond his right shoulder and his mind shot back decades towards the night when his mother's screams awoke him in the middle of the night. He remembered feeling paralysed listening to her panic as his father spoke what he believed to be gibberish.

After the tiny, sliced body was removed from the kitchen by the emergency services, Sean recalled his mother coming into his room to tell him Daddy and Rebecca had gone away for a while and both he and his mother would have to go stay with some family friends for a few weeks. Being the age he was, he didn't have any real need to query the reason his sister and father had gone away so he did as his mother asked.

It wasn't until a number of years following his sister's burial and the death of his father, Sean learned the full extent of what occurred in his house that night. His mother wanted him to have as normal a childhood as possible before cutting the rope on the tonne on bricks dangling over his head in relation to coming to terms with what his father had done. She told Sean she felt an older mind would be able to handle the truth better than a young one.

Taking another sip of whiskey, Sean's mind skipped to memories of his father. Sean had nothing but fond and fun memories of his youth up until several months before his sister's murder. His father always spent time with him and when his sister was born, he remembered him cradling Rebecca every chance he could get.

Many times, Sean had contemplated what had possessed his father to carry out such a heinous act and the more he thought about it over the years, the more his mind seemed to hurt. His father had no obvious motivation for murdering his daughter only that he had some kind a mental breakdown. It was extremely hard for Sean to come to terms with what his father had done. Known in the wider community, Thomas was often described as a hardworking, devoted man who loved his family dearly.

It was one night Sean remembered when he noted a big change in his father's behaviour. It was approximately eight in the evening when Thomas burst in through the back door of the house covered from head to toe in muck.

"What happened to you, are you okay?" Susan asked, grabbing the tea towel to wipe his stressed face.

"Yes I'm fine, one of the cows got into trouble out there. Spent ages trying to get it free and got destroyed in the process," Thomas said, wiping the muck from his face with the back of his hand.

"Jesus, you are freezing," Susan said, switching on the kettle to prepare a cup of soup for him.

Meanwhile, Thomas continued to wipe the mud from the palms of his hands while smiling towards his young son Sean sitting opposite him at the table doing his homework.

However, the boy couldn't help but notice the expression in his father's eyes. Although smiling towards him, the boy sensed a fear and concern in his father's stare.

"Here you go, get this into you. It'll help warm you," Susan said, placing a steaming cup of soup into the man's hands.

"Thank you," he said, turning to her, placing the hot beverage before his lips, and blowing on the liquid in front of him.

"So, what happened out there?" Susan asked.

"I heard the animal in distress while I was tiding up for the evening. I went to check on her, she had gotten herself tangled up in bushes and briers, so I spent some time working her out of it," he responded; his explanation vague.

However, she didn't query him any further on the topic and decided to let him get some heat back into his body unhindered.

Later that evening, Sean and his mother sat in the sitting room enjoying a board game while Thomas stayed in the kitchen eating his dinner.

"I'm going to get a drink Mammy," Sean, standing to his feet and walked towards the kitchen.

Pushing open the door, he noticed his father holding the window curtain to one side staring out into the darkness beyond the glass. Sean stood there a moment unnoticed by his father, who had a look of fear drawn across his face in the reflection.

"Oh, sorry son I didn't see you there," Thomas said, startled after spotting him at the corner of his eye, "everything okay?"

"Just getting a drink, what were you looking at?" the boy asked.

"Oh nothing, I was just seeing if it was still raining," his father replied walking over to the fridge and fetching a litre of milk.

"So how is school going for you?" Thomas asked as he poured his son a glass of milk.

"Good thanks," the young boy replied.

Suddenly there was a loud bang outside which caused Thomas to almost leap from his skin and quickly turned back to the window.

"What's that?" Sean asked, placing the cool glass quickly back onto the table, staring blankly at the window.

"It's nothing, don't worry. Go back inside to your mother," Thomas instructed.

"But-"

"Just do as I ask please," Thomas commanded in a firm tone.

Sean did as instructed and returned to the sitting room. Meanwhile, Thomas pulled open a kitchen drawer and grabbed one of the sharp knives from inside. He reached for the curtain, pulled it aside once more and peered into the thick blackness. He couldn't see anything except his own reflection in the glass.

Moving to the kitchen door, he gently unlocked it and slowly stepped out into the night. Turning, he noticed the wheelie bin which always sat beneath the kitchen window had fallen over. He quickly glanced around the area and nothing else seemed to be out of place. Breathing heavily, he walked towards the overturned bin.

"Thomas?" Susan called from the doorway, which caused him to jump again with fright in front of her.

"Jesus, you scared the life out of me," He said, turning to her, his knuckles white from holding the knife handle so tightly.

"Is everything okay?" she asked, as she stepped out into the yard.

"Yeah, yeah everything is fine," he responded, with his unarmed palm facing her, gesturing her to stay back from him.

Thomas turned and placed the blade on the ground beside him, grabbed the bin handles, and lugged the bin back to an upright position.

"Why did you bring a knife out with you?" his wife asked, as concern injected its way into her expression.

"Oh, I was going to cut some bread before I heard the bin fall over, I forgot I brought it out with me," he lied.

"What happened?" she asked.

"It must have been loaded to one side or

something, nothing to worry about," he smiled in an effort to stop the questioning.

The response eased her concern as he stepped towards her.

Hugging her he said, "Come on let's go back inside. I need to grab a shower anyway and it's freezing out here."

She returned to the sitting room and just before Thomas relocked the back door, he peered into the darkness once again to ensure everything was okay.

Taking the final sip of whiskey from his glass, Sean always wondered about the unusual behaviour of his father that evening, and what had his father so scared and what had he been looking for outside their house. Following his trip down memory lane, Sean looked towards the clock dangling on the wall above the mantelpiece as the fire below it faded to a glowing ash.

Standing to his feet, Sean decided to call it a night and went to ensure all the doors and windows were secure. Happy everything was switched off and the fire guard was in place, he retired to bed.

Chapter 4

Exhaling deeply after the day's work, Stephen turned to smile at his children playing chase with each other behind him. Watching the pair whizz around the yard brought great joy to the family man. Climbing down from the ladder after sealing the final piece around the fascia board, he placed the tools to one side and said, "Where do you two get the energy from?" As they bolted past him once again.

They responded with joyous laughter.

"Okay guys, time to get cleaned up," Stephen instructed.

"Can we stay out another while?" Owen asked.

"Yeah can we? Can we go see what that is?" His brother John added pointing towards the ominous landmark in the distance which had been the source of intrigue since moving there.

"Yeah can we?" Owen asked.

"No, you remember what Mr. Byrne said don't you?" his words instantly creating a look of disappointment on each boy's face. Stephen, although he wouldn't admit it, wanted to investigate the unusual landmark himself, only he hadn't had the time to go have a look around it. Thinking their dinner wouldn't be ready for at least another hour and looking at the excitement dissipate on their little faces, he pushed open the front door.

"When will dinner be ready love?" he called into the kitchen.

"About five, why?" Louise answered.

"The kids and I are going to go for a walk, we won't be long though," Stephen replied.

"Okay, enjoy," Louise shouted back through the house.

Shutting the door, Stephen spun to see the pair throwing a ball to each other, faster and faster as the seconds rolled by.

"Okay, come on you little rascals, time for an adventure," Stephen said, patting each of them on top of their hats. Walking past the boys, he opened his van door and retrieved a torch from the door pocket. He decided to go and have a look around the mound and thought it would be safe for the boys to go also because he would be with them.

John quickly followed, and not wanting to leave the football behind, Owen brought it with him, bouncing it off the road as they walked towards the field entrance just a short distance away.

By then the darkness had subtly began to massage the countryside around them as the lights of the houses began to twinkle on the hills in the distance.

Opening the gate, Stephen guided the children inside before closing it firmly behind them. Without warning, Owen kicked the ball along the grass in front of them and the two boys quickly gave chase, each wanting to beat the other to it first. Both full of excitement, knowing where they were going.

"Careful now boys," Stephen said, taking note of the evening dew building up on the surface beneath them, trying to light as much as the field as possible with the torch.

Their giddy laughter came in response.

Moving through the field, Stephen turned his attention to the mound in the distance which seemed to pulsate within the ever-thickening darkness. He put this effect down to it being at the forefront of the twilight sky in the background. Beautiful, he said to himself as they neared the unusual piece of land.

Stepping closer, it seemed to hypnotically grab the children's attention as well, Owen gently tapping the football before him as they journeyed to their destination.

An eerie silence befell the land as they stopped a few feet from the enclosed area. The trio momentarily stood in awe of the sight.

"What is it?" John asked, stepping a little closer.

"I don't know," his father replied, equally intrigued.

"Can we go in?" Owen added to the conversation.

"No, remember what mister Byrne said? It's too dangerous for us to go in there," Stephen reaffirmed, thinking he was already being a little cocky having been in the field without permission.

Looking into the dense undergrowth, Stephen wished he had left sooner as by then very little could be seen through it, even with the help of the strong torchlight.

They stepped around the perimeter, while Owen gently kicked the ball behind them.

"We should have come up when it was bright. Maybe it was a little silly coming up during the evening eh?" Stephen laughed, nudging John, who smiled in return.

"Can we come back during the day?" Owen asked, while his father turned to ensure he was still close to them.

"We'll see," Stephen replied, bringing a smile to the boy's face.

"I wonder what is in there," John said, looking up to the tall trees sprouting from behind the clay mound surrounding them.

"Okay let's go back, dinner is probably ready by now," the boy's father instructed.

Instantly John jogged towards the gate at the far side of the field.

"Careful John," Stephen instructed.

Seeing his brother running away, Owen kicked the football towards him to begin their game once more. John turned, stopped the ball, and adjusted his position. With a thump he returned the ball to his brother, however, it hit a divot on the ground, ricocheted between Owen and his father, and bounced straight into the dark hedge line behind them.

Instantly Owen's face dropped watching the football disappear before him.

"I'll get it," John said, running back towards the pair.

"No... no I will, you both stay here," Stephen instructed once John reached them.

Both children did as they were told and turned to watch their father walk towards the tiny opening in the ditch which the ball had created. Although being warned not to go in there by the land owner, Stephen couldn't walk home with disappointed children and plus he thought to himself it would only take two minutes to find it and the children could leave happy.

As Stephen stepped towards the ominous landmark, the torchlight shone brightly before him like a batten trying to keep the thickening darkness at bay.

Climbing through the heavy ditch made up of branches, briars and a small mud incline, he instantly noticed a thicker darkness inside. Within moments, an unusual dizziness fell upon Stephen as the smell of freshly dug earth filled his nostrils. The boys looked on as they watched the torch's light frantically swipe from side to side.

As Stephen peered around the enclosure aided by the light cast from the torch, he tried to figure out what was happening to him. Time slowed to a snail's pace as he became even more disorientated.

"Daddy?" came the muffled call from the children outside the dubious enclosure.

"It's okay, stay there," he slurred in response, his head beginning to vibrate and vision becoming blurry due to the pain.

Noticing the interwoven trees, he began to feel nauseous and it was then he eyed a stomach-churning sight.

Focusing the beam in between two tree trunks a short distance away, Stephen spotted two barefooted feet which immediately struck him as odd. They donned a pale skin colour and about halfway up the inside of each foot was another long toe. Concentrating as much as he could through the sensory bombardment, he shone the light upwards. Stephens's eyes widened even further when he witnessed the skinny, topless torso, long jagged black hair, abnormally long arms, and hands which appeared to have extremely long claw like features. The creature was approximately three feet tall, however, once he made eye contact, he couldn't turn away from the two balls of bright white glaring from behind the thick hair covering this creature's face.

"You disturbed us," hissed a voice slowly toward Stephen.

"Dad?" John called once more, wondering why the light had suddenly stopped followed by waves of crashing silence.

"Stay where you are, everything is okay," Stephen shouted.

"What are you?" Stephen asked.

"You don't belong here, you disturbed us. There is a price for what you've done," was the reply as one hideous creature was joined by another, then another until there were countless, unblinking eyes staring at him.

Stephen began to wince in pain as they stepped out from the cover of the undergrowth. Turning he could see even more of them clawing their way from the soil and making their way towards him. Some were bald, with only single strands of hair sprouting from their head in limited places, while others had a full head of extremely long hair. He could see each face had a flat surface where a nose should be and each creature had a jagged mouth, with sharp fangs bursting passed their uneven lips

"Get out!" a voice roared as he collapsed to the ground and began quickly crawling back the way he came.

Reaching the boundary of this home to unnatural beasts, his right leg was clawed viciously before he managed to escape by quickly grabbing the ground and pulling his way out to the other side.

"Dad, you okay?" John asked, racing over to his father. "What happened in there?"

"I'm okay, don't worry I just fell," Stephen replied, trying not to cause alarm, looking back at the mound to make sure he wasn't followed, while still trying to figure out what had just happened.

It was clear the boys hadn't heard the full confrontation inside and he wanted to get out of there as quickly as possible. "Come on, let's get back to the house," he said climbing to unsteady feet as the blood began to splash against the wet grass beneath him.

"Did you find the ball?" Owen innocently asked, while he and John looked on in horror at the wound on Stephen's leg.

"No, but we need to back home now okay?" Stephen instructed as calmly as he could, placing an arm around each boy, moving away from the scene as fast as he could, holding the torch in his right hand, to guide them.

Rushing towards the gate, Stephen glanced back every few moments to ensure none of the creatures he had encountered were pursuing them.

When they were about halfway between the road and the mound, countless scurrying footsteps through the damp grass could be heard all around them.

"What is that Daddy?" John asked, as he looked around the growing darkness trying to find the source of the noises circling them.

"It's nothing, don't worry about it," Stephen said, pulling the children closer to him. "Just keep moving, we're almost there." He could see the kitchen light in the distance getting closer; Louise inside unaware of the pulsating terror bombarding her husband and children.

The footsteps seemed to grow heavier and closer the further they moved through the thick, wet grass, causing the sweat to fall even quicker from Stephen's brow. Stephen's wound caused him to limp harder in agony as he tried to quicken up the pace to get his children away from whatever evil he had awoken.

A sudden silence collided against their ears when they reached the gate. Stephen quickly unlatched it and ushered Owen and John onto the road, turning to close it, a sinister whisper floated through the darkness towards Stephen. "Give us the children!" Stephen froze in terror. Staring into the empty blackness, breathing heavily and fists clenched, he looked for any sign of advancement towards them. Even though he was wounded, he would defend them to the death.

"Leave us alone you hear me!" he roared into the dead night air.

No response came as he swiftly shone the torch around in front of him.

His attention quickly turned to his petrified children standing behind him.

"Let's get inside," Stephen instructed, placing his arms around the pair once again and walking them towards the house.

Reaching the front door, the boy's father opened it and rushed them inside. They were instantly hit with the aroma of evening's dinner being dished up for them. Louise heard them coming in and began serving their meal, thinking they would be hungry after their walk. Stephen quickly closed and locked the door.

"Mammy, Mammy," Owen cried, as he ran through the sitting room into the small kitchen.

"Everything okay?" Louise asked, as the young child wrapped his arms around her with a tight grip.

"Daddy's hurt."

Lifting her head, she saw Stephen collapsing into his favourite chair in the sitting room. Her eyes widened and her concern skyrocketed when she saw the damage to his leg and the blood pouring from the large lacerations.

"Stephen what happened?" Louise asked, as she raced to her husband.

He briefly considered telling her what he had seen within the rath but thought better of it as he didn't want to cause any further panic until he knew exactly what he was dealing with.

"Something followed us home," John quickly said, adding to Louise's concern.

"What's going on Stephen?" she asked as she lifted the leg of his pants, revealing the deep wounds.

"Nothing, I think it was a fox behind us. That must be what we heard," he continued, trying to contain his fear and attempting to stem his family's distress.

"So, it was a fox that did this to your leg? They look like claw marks."

"Yeah, it was dark and it all happened so quickly, maybe I stumbled on its den and it was protecting it," was the explanation he managed to weave together quickly.

"Okay well we need to clean this and stop the bleeding," Louise said standing to her feet.

She went back into the kitchen and began filling a basin with warm water, meanwhile Stephen called

Owen and John to him. Looking into the children's eyes, he could sense their fear and confusion about what they had just been through.

"Daddy had a silly accident, but everything is fine okay?" he said to the two pale faces in front of him.

"But something chased us," John replied.

"Don't worry, it was just a fox. There is nothing to worry about, you know I'd never let anything happen to you both." he smiled to his boys.

He pulled them close and gave each a long hug.

"Okay, give me a second and I'll have a look at that," Louise said, placing the basin down beside him. "Go have some dinner while I look after Daddy," she said to the children, who did as they were told as she followed them back to the kitchen.

She returned to Stephen with towels and a first aid kit. Folding a large towel, she placed it on the floor beneath him to help catch the blood flowing from his leg. Louise knelt on one knee and took hold of Stephens's leg and carefully placed it on top of her thigh, causing him to grimace with pain.

"Okay, hold still," she said opening the first aid box.

Retrieving the scissors, she carefully cut in a straight line up along his jeans, away as much as possible from the jagged indents in his leg.

"Oh no, not my good jeans," he grinned, trying to ease the tension of the situation a little, for his sake as much as hers.

"Shush you," she smiled.

Stopping at his right knee, she cut the waste piece off exposing the full extent of the damage. Louise dipped a towel into the basin and pressed in against the cuts, causing Stephen to grit his teeth and the leg to vibrate in agony.

"These are very deep, you may need stitches and a tetanus injection," Louise told him as she kept dabbing and wiping. "I don't know how you were able to walk so far on it. A doctor should look at them either way to make sure you don't get an infection."

"I'll go tomorrow, it's too late now," Stephen replied, knowing it was the combination of adrenaline and getting his children to safety which had aided him to get through the immense pain.

"I can take you to the hospital now," Louise continued.

"No please, I just want to rest, I promise I'll go tomorrow," Stephen confirmed.

"Typical man," Louise smiled. "Okay well don't leave it too long, we'll go first thing okay?"

He nodded in reply.

Louise then took some disinfectant wipes from the box beside her. She wiped the wounds, and preparing himself for the immense sting, Stephen squeezed the armrests harder with each wipe. Finally, Louise took a large bandage and pressed it against the lacerations with one hand, then with the other, she wrapped it firmly around his leg.

While his wife bandaged his leg, Stephen couldn't

get the hideous figures out of his mind. Staring at the dark kitchen window from the sitting room, he was trying to control his nerves, looking at the glass, all he could visualise in his mind were countless white eyes staring back at him and smashing their way inside. To his relief, the image remained just a part of his imagination and he turned to his wife once more who was finishing wrapping his leg. Looking at her, Stephen again considered telling her everything that had happened, but he just couldn't bring himself to do it and more so, he wasn't sure if he could even explain the experience himself. What are they? He thought as he looked around the room for a weapon just in case the door or windows were kicked in at any moment, because he knew whatever they were, they had followed them, and must surely know now he lives in the house beside the field.

"All done," Louise said as she stood, bringing Stephen's attention back to his wife.

"Thank you," he smiled.

"Remember, doctors first thing tomorrow okay?" she replied.

"I am always in good hands with you, aren't I?" he said taking her hand in his.

"Someone has to look after you boys," she said, giving him a kiss on the cheek.

For the remainder of the evening, Stephen tried his best to interact with his family as normal as he could while keeping close attention on the doors and windows for any sign of those hideous creatures breaking in to finish off the job they had started on him. What tortured him more than the thought of what they could do to him, was the thought of how vulnerable his family would be without him there to protect them.

"Was it really a fox Daddy?" John asked later that night, as his father tucked him into bed.

"Yes, it was. Don't worry, everything is fine," Stephen replied, placing a reassuring hand on the child's forehead. "Now get some sleep okay," he said, as he walked to the door and flicked off the light switch, John's concern settling a little with his answer.

"Are they alright?" Louise asked, as Stephen returned to the sitting room.

"Yeah just a little shaken that's all," he said, sitting down beside her.

"They're not the only ones," she said, turning to him.

"Don't worry, it'll take more than that to put me down," he grinned, as he placed his arm around her.

The couple watched television together before going to bed. Before joining his wife in the bedroom, Stephen double checked around the house to ensure all access points were fully closed and locked. There was no way he wanted those beasts to get into the house during the night, even though he was confident he wasn't going to get any sleep after what he had witnessed.

Lifting the blind to check the kitchen window, he looked in the direction of where he had sustained the wounds on his leg. He studied for any sign of movement towards the cottage. After a few moments, he lowered the blind and finished his checks on the house, once satisfied he limbered to Louise in the bedroom. He considered getting the family into his van and driving away as quickly as possible but thought to himself that it may not do any good, as they would have to come back at some stage.

Pushing open the door, he could hear her gentle breathing as she enjoyed her peaceful slumber. He hated that he hadn't been honest with her, however he felt it was for the best until he knew exactly what he had encountered, unknowing that Louise had already experienced something strange at that ominous place beside their land.

Stephen climbed into bed and lay on his back staring at the ceiling for a number of hours while the pain of his injuries injected their way through his leg, listening to every little creak and movement within the tiny cottage. After some time, his mind became exhausted and he drifted off to sleep.

Chapter 5

The following morning Stephen awoke to the cheerful chirps of birds playing on the roof above his bedroom, as the rays of sunlight collided against the still drawn curtains. The smell of fried meat weaved its way into the bedroom causing his mouth to water however, the reality of the previous evening quickly shot through him once he moved his leg slightly in the bed.

Wincing as he pulled himself slowly upright, he swung the blankets to one side and spun gently on the mattress until his feet touched the carpet beneath him. Sitting on the edge of the bed, he looked down to his heavily bandaged leg, which had grown more painful overnight, and immediately thought of those horrid creatures once more. His mind turned to how he was going to manage getting back to work. He was already missing that Monday however, he didn't want to be out of action too long.

Climbing to his feet, he dressed himself, pulled back the curtains to reveal a beautiful day displayed before him. He limped to the bedroom door and made his way through the sitting room, into the adjoining kitchen.

"Morning sleepy head," Louise said, as she placed his breakfast on the plate. "I didn't want to wake you, it looked like you needed the rest," she smiled.

"What time is it?" he yawned.

"Just gone nine. How's the leg?" she asked, placing the frying pan back onto the cooker.

"Killing me," he laughed, "but I'll manage."

"Well get that into you and then we are going to the doctor."

"Okay, but I don't want to make a big fuss out of it, I want to get back to work as soon as I can. Did the kids get off to school alright?" Stephen asked, lifting the cup of tea to his mouth.

"Yeah, they did, they were still a little rattled from last night though. Are you sure there isn't anything else you want to tell me?" Louise asked in a concerned tone, noting to herself something unusual had happened when she was up at that place and now her husband had sustained a serious injury while wandering around up there.

"Ah, I think they just got a fright when they saw the blood that's all. There is nothing to worry about. I just need to get this looked at and get back on my feet properly," he replied.

"What's more important now, your work or your leg?" Louise quickly shot back, knowing he was a workaholic and couldn't sit easy if he knew there was work to be done.

"I know… I know," He grinned back to his wife, looking at the love she had for him displayed in her eyes. "I'll ring Dave and tell him I'll be out for a few days. He can look after the project until I get back."

"Well that is what you pay him for isn't it? He is a foreman after all. And stop that few days' nonsense, you'll rest as long as the doctor tells you to you hear me Stephen McKenna!" she said, turning to the sink to begin the washing up.

Stephen didn't bother arguing because he knew by her tone Louise wasn't taking no for an answer.

After finishing his breakfast, Stephen struggled to his feet and followed his wife to their car.

The couple reached the doctor's surgery after a half a hour trek over the winding countryside. Parking as close to the door as possible in the tiny village, Louise helped her husband from the car and aided him towards reception.

After speaking with the receptionist, they were asked to take a seat until Doctor O' Neill was finished seeing his current patient. Stephen wore a pair of shorts he usually wears during the summer on site to allow easy access to the torn leg. Looking down at the bandages, which were stained red over the lacerations, Stephen hoped after seeing the doctor it would be the end to the nightmarish reality of visiting the circular structure in the fields beside his house. Once on the mend, he would ensure his family never went near that place again and vowed to query Sean. He has to know something about that place and what they are! Stephen thought to himself as the doctor's office door opened.

After saying farewell to the elderly lady patient, whom had been in with him for a check up on her arm which was in a sling, the doctor turned and said "Stephen." While beckoning him into the room.

Louise stood, helped her husband to his feet, and followed the doctor into his office.

"Well I was going to ask what I can do for you, but I think that's a little obvious, can you sit down here?" Doctor O' Neill said, as he took up his position on the small stool beside the bed across from his desk.

Stephen did as he was asked and winced slightly as he lowered himself onto the blanket.

"Okay go ahead and lie down for me," The doctor said, pulling the stool closer as Stephen spun on his bottom, lifting his legs onto the bed. "This looks fresh, want to tell me what happened?"

"I was out walking last night and I fell, it was dark, I don't really know, maybe a fox clawed me too," Stephen quickly replied through gritted teeth as the doctor began to remove the bandages from around his leg.

"Really?" The doctor replied, inquisitive eyes turning towards Louise.

"Yeah really," Stephen confirmed.

"Okay," the doctor said as he revealed the torn skin beneath the damp, bloodied bandages. "Thankfully the bleeding has mostly stopped," he said, examining the large crimson tears. "Well, I can tell you for sure a fall didn't do this, you would have a lot more injuries from an impact needed to cause these," the doctor continued.

Louise quickly turned to Stephen looking for an explanation.

"Like I said, I fell, but it was dark, and I think a fox done it. I don't know, maybe I scared it or something," Stephen stuttered the answer as best he could.

The look on the Doctor O' Neill's face was enough to tell Louise he thought the explanation was a bit of a stretch.

"Okay, well these are deep and going to need stitches I'm afraid," he said.

Spinning on the stool, Doctor O' Neill stood and went to the hand basin beside his desk. After washing his hands, he pulled a glove over each hand and reached into the drawer on the medical utensil bench beside the sink. From it he retrieved two syringes, two vials of liquid, a needle and thread, disinfectant wipes, and a pair of scissors.

He placed the items onto a small stainless-steel bench and wheeled it over to the bed on which Stephen was lying.

Taking his position once more on the stool, he reached for the first vile and the syringe.

"I'm going to give you a tetanus injection and something for the pain," the doctor said, preparing the shot.

"Okay," Stephen replied. He was thankful to hear that, because in his mind he had no idea what filth lay beneath the claws of the creature which had attacked him and what infections may develop from the wounds.

After injecting the medicine, followed by another injection used around various edges of the wounds to help numb them, the doctor said, "Ready?" He proceeded to clean around Stephens's leg with the wipes. This caused the man's knuckles to turn white as he gripped the mattress tightly and stared at the ceiling hoping for the immense stinging to cease as soon as possible.

Once satisfied the wounds were clean, Doctor O' Neill threaded the needle, checked on Stephen once again, who confirmed he couldn't feel anything, and began to pull the torn pieces of skin back together.

It was a strange sensation for Stephen feeling the pressure of the needle piercing his skin and the tightness it caused as each laceration was sewn together.

The process took about half an hour before the doctor sat upright and gave Stephens's leg a number of more rubs with disinfectant and then stood to his feet.

"Okay that should do it," Doctor O' Neill said, pulling each glove off by the cuff and placing them into the medical waste bin.

"How long until I can go back to work?" Stephen queried, as he spun around and slowly placed his foot to the floor.

"I want you back in ten days to take out the stitches. I don't recommend working at all until then and even after they have been removed, you'll have to take extreme care to prevent them from opening," the doctor explained, as he stepped over to a tiny store room at the opposite side of his office. From it he retrieved a pair of crutches. "These should help you get around a little easier for the next couple of days," the doctor continued, making some adjustments, before handing them to Stephen so he could stand to his feet.

"Thanks," Stephen said, attaching a crutch to each arm, not liking the thoughts of being off work for the next two to three weeks. He was a driven man and the idea of sitting around waiting for his leg to heal was already wearing on him. The doctor monitored Stephen's movements for a few moments and made some final adjustment to the crutches.

"Just get plenty of rest and over the counter pain killers are sufficient as you need them," Doctor O' Neill said, stepping over to the door and opening it for the couple.

"Thank you," Louise said, as she walked with her husband back towards reception to agree payment and to make an appointment to get the stitches out.

Journeying back home Stephen couldn't get the events from the previous night out of his mind and also the warning Sean had given the family to stay away from that place. He must know something. Stephen thought to himself as he dazed at the countryside passing by him on the opposite side of the glass.

"Can you drop me off at Sean's place on the way

back?" Stephen asked his wife.

"Is everything okay, shouldn't you be resting?" she replied as she manoeuvred the car along the winding, narrow country road, thinking it was a little unusual to be visiting the farmer in his condition.

"Yeah everything is fine don't worry. I just want to have a chat with him about this," he said pointing to his leg. "I don't want him thinking we are going to try and cause any trouble for him."

"That makes sense I suppose, at some stage it may get back to him it happened on his land. But can't it wait until you are better?" Louise asked, getting the car as close to the ditch as possible to allow the one coming from the opposite direction to pass safely by them.

"I'd prefer to do it now," Stephen responded.

After another ten-minute drive, the couple arrived at the entrance to Sean's home.

"Are you sure you don't want me to come in with you? He might not even be home," Louise asked, as she watched her husband struggle from the car.

"No, I'll be fine, I'll ring you when I'm ready okay?" he said, turning to her.

"Okay, well watch that leg and don't be too long. You're supposed to be resting," his visibly disapproving wife reminded him.

Stephen smiled, closed the door, and began to make his way up the old dirt driveway which had a strip of grass pushing its way up through the clay and running up the middle of it towards the old farm house.

Swinging forward gingerly on the crutches, Stephen wanted answers to what was lurking in that field and he was confident Sean would have them for him.

Resting in his sitting room, the window of which faced towards the small country road, Sean heard the clinking of the crutches against the dirt making their way closer to his property. Standing, he looked outside and saw his injured neighbour approaching the front door.

"Stephen what on earth happened to you?" the retired farmer asked, swinging open the heavy wooden door.

"How are you Sean, do you mind if I come in? I need to have a chat with you," Stephen said, as he eased his right foot onto the ground.

"Of course, come on in. I'll put the kettle on," the elderly man said, standing aside, holding the door open so Stephen could pass by. "Make yourself at home," he added.

The sitting room sat between the kitchen, which was to the right and the corridor to the bedrooms was to the left.

Stephen did so as Sean stepped into the kitchen to fetch them a cup of tea.

Resting himself onto the large couch, Stephen glanced around the room which had a vast showcase of both coloured and black and white photographs proudly displayed on its walls. The mantelpiece supported many different sized ornaments and beneath the window sat a small table with numerous magazines and books placed neatly upon it. Looking out to the trees swaying gently in the breeze, he wondered how he was going to turn the conversation towards what exactly happened to his leg and what he had encountered in that field.

"Here you go," Sean said, walking to the room, handing the cup to Stephen, interrupting his thoughts. "Jesus, that looks serious enough, happen at work?" Sean continued, as he lowered himself into the old, soft chair across from the injured man.

"No," Stephen said, wanting to burst into asking him what the hell is in that place? But he didn't want to be so abrupt, so he bit his tongue and instead asked, "Listen I have to ask, why were you so insistent no one was to set foot into the circular mound out there in the fields?"

Sean instantly stopped sipping his tea and stared at Stephen. A few, long, silence filled seconds dragged by as each man looked towards the other until Sean responded with, "I just don't want anyone getting hurt that's all."

"What put it there, is it man made?" Stephen quickly asked.

"Honestly, I'm not sure. But why do you ask? Is this to do with your leg?" with a tremor in his voice, the farmer asked, as he looked down towards the heavily bandaged limb.

Stephen knew there was no point sugar-coating his

reason for being there any further and decided to get to the point, "Yes, it is. I decided to take the kids for a walk yesterday evening so we went up to the thing at the top of the field. Anyway, I had to go in and this happened," the injured man explained.

"You went inside? I told you never to do that!" Sean said, with widening eyes.

"Something did this to me when I was trying to get out, something spoke to me, and didn't want me there," Stephen said, studying Sean's face growing paler by the second. "You know what they are don't you? Tell me what that place is!"

"I don't know what they are because I've never set foot in there, never!" Sean said, sitting forward in the chair. "My father grew an unhealthy obsession with that place and after he did what he did, he blamed them for it."

"Them? What did he do?" Stephen couldn't help but ask.

Sean paused a moment, he considered if he should reveal what his father done many years ago.

"Sean?" Stephen asked once more.

"He murdered my infant sister right there in the kitchen. After he butchered her, he blamed them and said it wasn't even her he had killed. He was sent to prison and there he died. He claimed it's a fairy ring, wrath, or whatever you want to call it, and he had disturbed them, and they took their revenge on him." Sean said, knowing that Stephen would eventually find out one way or another.

Stephen sat motionless while he listened to the shocking information. Sean took a sip of his warm drink and continued, "He isn't the only one who claims it is a home to the fairies, many around here won't go near the place."

"Why the hell didn't you tell us about any of this before?" Stephen erupted, confusion still ricocheting through him as he tried to process what he had been told.

"Because if I had told you what my father believed and others around here believe that place to be, it would have created more interest in it for you to go up there don't you think? Plus, I don't know what to believe myself. All that can't be real right?" Sean said.

"Well this is real and whatever did it to me is real," Stephen shot venomously back pointing to his leg. "So what you're saying is people believe it is a fairy ring, and if you disturb them they seek revenge? So, what happens now?" he asked in disbelief, thinking to himself that in no way fairies can be real but something horrid had indeed clawed at his leg.

Sean wanted to challenge him about being on his land, however he decided against it and replied with, "I really don't know. I don't know what to tell you, my mother said my father murdered her child and was only using excuses to try get away with it in terms of insanity and the others around here are old and very superstitious."

"Listen, I'm sorry, I didn't mean to snap at you. I just find it hard to believe that little fairies did this to me. Something vicious was up there though and there was more than one of them," Stephen said, taking a deep inhale.

"No need to be sorry. Did you get a look at them?" Sean asked, listening attentively for a response.

"I did, but I really don't know what I saw. I wanted to know if this had happened to anyone up there before and if you had any idea what it was. I've more questions now than when I came in," the injured man said, placing his hand over his face and rubbing his eyes.

"I know what you mean. I've always had questions about that place ever since my father did what he did all those years ago but my mother would never let me near the place and over the years, I decided to stay away from it," Sean added.

Feeling his leg begin to pulsate with pain, Stephen decided to stop the questioning for the day and go home to get more pain killers into his system. He thanked Sean for giving him his time then phoned Louise to come and collect him.

Once Stephen left his home, Sean sat in the comfortable sitting room chair for some time contemplating what his visitor had told him, was my father right all along? He thought as he looked out through the window, the daylight beginning to fade across the beautiful, serene countryside.

Pulling himself up to his feet, he walked over to the old, large fireplace and pulled back the fire guard.

As he cleaned the ashes from the night before, Sean glanced towards a picture he had always held so dearly in his heart. It was an old, framed, black and white photo of his parents, Thomas and Susan, holding him in the very room he was standing in when he was an infant. Looking at his father's contagious smile, he wondered, like he had over the many years, what had driven him to murder his daughter.

Introducing a flame to the firelighters, Sean tossed a few lumps of coal around them, then settled a dry log on top and watched the fire begin to take hold.

Satisfied, he stepped into the kitchen, retrieved a small glass, and sat it upon the table, he turned and went to the freezer. He placed three ice cubes into the glass and fetched himself a bottle of his favourite whiskey which he always kept stocked in the house.

Returning to the sitting room, the fire now ablaze, Sean sat down, poured the fine liquid from the bottle into the glass, took a sip, and savoured the taste.

Staring into the flames, he remembered the screams of his mother the night she found her daughter stabbed to death in the kitchen he had just been in. So many times over the years he tried to decipher what had possessed his father to carry out such a horrific act, and so many times no conclusion could be found other than that he had simply lost his mind.

Enjoying another sip of the fine beverage, he remembered his father's rant saying they had driven him to it, and he had no choice but to kill her. Could there really be something living behind that mound full of dense brush and trees?

Sean poured himself another glass and began to enjoy it immediately.

Remembering Stephen's account from earlier, made the old farmer wonder what was off about that weird structure on his land and why was it associated with bad events. So many times he had wanted to march up to the ring fort, venture inside to reassure himself it was just that, a fort from times long past and nothing more, then kick himself for being so silly in the first place.

Watching the warm, dancing, hypnotic flames building in front of him, he continued to savour the strong beverage.

Stephen's story would have sounded far-fetched to anyone on its own, the farmer thought to himself, however when accompanied with the fears of other locals in the area and the actions of his father so many years ago, it was slowly starting to confirm to Sean maybe his father wasn't so crazy after all and there just might be something lurking out in those fields.

Splashing another generous amount of whiskey into the empty glass, Sean stood and added more firewood to the red coal before him. The darkness outside had by then fully collapsed on the silent countryside. It had been quite some time since his chat with Stephen and peering towards the whiskey bottle sitting beside him, the bottle was just below halfway full. Feeling the effects of the alcohol taking hold of his body, Sean exhaled loudly, fetched the remote control, and turned on the television as the fire caused various shadows to dance around the room.

Flicking through the mundane evening programs, he couldn't get the visual image of the rath or what superstitious people called, a fairy ring, out of his mind, it was niggling him, slowly bombarding him.

Stephen's story ran through the farmer's mind once more while he remembered the injured man pointing towards the wound on his leg. I have to check! Sean finally thought to himself.

The elderly man downed the last of the drink in his hand and pulled himself to his feet. Sean had always been cautious of that place ever since his traumatic childhood experience and his father's stern warnings. Truth be known he had had countless nightmares about that piece of land and what his father's obsession had done to his family. It was time to step inside the place he was told to stay out of, to see once and for all if there was indeed was something lurking within it.

Although the night was calm and dry, it was still very cold, so he pulled on a large coat around his aging body and doubled up his socks on each foot. Stepping into the kitchen, Sean retrieved a large torch from one of the many kitchen cupboards. Walking over to the kitchen door, he pushed down on the handle to ensure the door was locked. Moving back through the sitting room, he made sure the fire was safe, and then collected and pulled on the time worn Wellingtons standing by the front door.

Stepping out, he eyed his exhaled breath before him as he turned to lock the door behind him. Instead of walking along the road to the field entrance beside Stephen and Louise's house, he decided to travel through the adjoining fields. It would be quicker and also it wouldn't cause alarm, as his neighbours may see the bright light wondering close to their property otherwise.

Stepping to his left, the farmer opened the tiny gate and made his way through the little farm yard which had a small grouping of sheds and the rusting remains of a tractor his father used to use. Reaching the first field gate at the opposite side of the yard, he placed his withering hands on the old, cold steel handle, slid it to the right, swung the gate open, and stepped out onto the old cattle path the family used to take the former herd to and from the fields for milking.

Sean noticed his pace was slightly quicker than usual, clearly the mixture of fine Irish whiskey and air was influencing him. Strolling through the field, he wondered why it had taken him so long to do what he was doing, however his influenced mind didn't dwell on the thought too long reaching the next gate.

Entering the second large field, the fairy ring sat in the next. Reaching the next gate, he remembered the night he and his mother found his distressed father down on his knees in the torrential rain.

Shining the light down the huge pasture, Sean had to leave the cattle path and venture into the thick grass to reach the structure which had commanded the land for countless years, and by then, the people around it. Careful of his footing, the farmer set off in the general direction of the ring fort. Moving through the darkness, he noticed there was no small, twinkling lights shimmering in the distance which indicated to him Stephen and his family were in bed, so too was their next-door neighbour, Mary.

After slowly making his way through the field for approximately five minutes, the image of an earthen structure began to reveal itself at the edge of the torch light.

Nothing looked out of place in front of him as he moved closer to the landmark. A quick wisp of the night's chill brushed against his face as he shone the light slowly left and right across the mound and heavy brush.

Judgemental thoughts began to stroll into his mind, wondering why he had decided to inspect the apparent source of torment at such a late hour, but he had to be sure it was just the remains of times long ago and nothing more.

Stepping closer to the circumference of the structure, he listened closely, nothing could be heard only the occasional, gentle branch creak in the soft breeze.

Sean shone the light directly into the fairy ring and

stood silently, studying every twist and bend, torn and branch before him. Thinking of his father's warnings and the story Stephen had confessed to him earlier that day, he couldn't get his mind around to believing that fairies exist and live in places like the one before him around Ireland.

"They can't be real," he said as he reached out and touched one of the thick, heavy briars gently moving before him. Instantly, the temperature plummeted around him and thousands of inconceivable whispers filled his ears.

Sean quickly swiped the torch around him to try find the source, but nothing could be seen. Turning, disbelieving his ears, Sean realised the whispering was coming from within the fairy fort. The old farmer took one step back and said, "Who's there?"

Silence fell around him.

"I said, who is there!" Sean shouted in a more authoritative tone. Again there was no answer.

Thinking the tasty whiskey was having a greater effect on him, Sean reached forward and took hold of one of the thin outer branches. Still not fully giving in to the possibility to the existence of fairies, so many times, as like many Irish children growing up, he was always told to never disturb or take anything from the fairies.

Thinking of his father and Stephen, the old man wanted to know once and for all if there was something sinister lurking in or beneath the structure on his land. With a quick snap, Sean broke the small branch and pulled it from the heavy undergrowth.

Instantly Sean caught sight of numerous eyes upon him from the darkness within the fairy ring.

"Who are you, what are you doing on my land?" he called out, as more and more bright white pupils placed their unblinking gaze upon him.

"Sean…" a voice slowly floated towards him.

"Get out of here, you don't belong here," the elderly man said, as he started to slowly retreat.

"No, you are the one who doesn't belong here Sean, you disturbed us just like your father." A voice echoed slowly around him.

Without warning, countless creatures burst from their abode and surrounded the old farmer. Shining the light quickly from one horrendous face to the next, Sean could not take his eyes off the crooked fangs and pale eyes glaring at him.

"My father was right," Sean said, eyes widening with every passing moment, "you drove him to kill his own child."

"No, you are wrong old man," came the reply. Sean was unable to find the specific creature which was speaking to him. It was though all the fairies were projecting the sentences into his mind simultaneously while just staring at him. "This is your real sister."

One of the fairies turned and walked to the edge of the mound and shoved its thin arm deep into the mud. Moments later, the creature slowly pulled its long limb from the earth and with it came a small bundle of tattered cloth. Turning, the fairy faced him and unveiled a tiny, decomposed, human skeleton, with scattered strands of hair upon its small head.

"Say hello to your sister." The evil voice of the fairy infiltrated Sean's mind as he looked on in horror at the little remains being paraded in front of him.

"No, you're lying, she's buried in the cemetery. My father killed my sister because of you," the old man finally managed to squeeze past his lips.

"No, it wasn't your sister, we made him give her away. We took her from him for disturbing us and claimed her for ourselves. We watched her cry with hunger as she slowly rotted away and became this wretched thing," said the fairy, who was holding the corpse before tossing it to the ground at Sean's feet. "He was meant to raise the changeling as his own, knowing it wasn't his beautiful child, that's what his punishment was for disturbing us but as you know he was weak, pathetic and couldn't take the torment, so he killed the changeling when it was at its weakest."

"This can't be true!" the farmer replied, trying to process the new information given to him.

"It is, usually we never tell the parents when we have taken their child and swapped it for one of our own, but we couldn't resist watching your father tear himself and his family apart. Of course, when he killed the changeling, we had to make him suffer another way."

"His cancer?" Sean replied, his stomach slowly knotting tighter with each passing second.

All the creatures around him simultaneously shot a

sinister grin towards him as he shone the torch around the large group once again.

"No one ever gets away from us Sean, one way or another we will always make those who disturb or enter our world suffer as much as possible and now you have made the same mistake," they said, as they walked towards the farmer.

Sean turned and began for home as quickly as possible, the fairies followed.

Moving through the field, he could hear them swarming around him as sadistic whispering filled his ears, followed by the terrifying sounds of a newborn baby crying in agony. However, Sean knew it was impossible and they were just toying with him.

Suddenly, he was greeted by a wall of pale white eyes in front of him, "We can't let you leave Sean."

Seconds later, two claws wrapped around Sean's frail ankles and swiftly pulled them back and upwards. Slamming face first into the mud, Sean became disorientated. Having no time to gather himself, two more abnormally long arms reached for his wrists, stretched out his arms and held him in position, while several of the fairies climbed upon his back. Sean could feel the countless feet climbing on him, and then came the pain as they began to tear away at his back with their vicious sharp limbs.

Sean screamed in agony, however this was quickly combatted by another hand reaching out, grabbing his head and shoving his face hard into the dirt, causing the screams to become muffled cries for help.

The pain continued to speed through the old farmer, legs and arms rattling in anguish as the pieces of flesh were torn from his back. He was quickly turned over, by then he couldn't scream, he could only concentrate on the torture he had received.

Casting his eyes slightly to the right, blood soaking the grass beneath him as his life was slowly leaving his body, Sean witnessed one of the fairies walk towards and stand over him. Looking at the expressionless face, Sean knew his time had come. Without any hesitation, the long-haired fiend placed one jagged nailed hand over his mouth, and plunged its index finger on the other, deep into one side of his neck.

Staring into Sean's pain filled eyes, the fiend slowly pulled its embedded claw from left to right and the fairies watched as he died, alone on the cold ground beneath them.

"It took you long enough to finally visit us," a voice whispered slowly through the night air and in an instant all the fairies were gone.

Unaware of his neighbour's horrendous death, Stephen lay awake in his bed, arm firmly wrapped around Louise.

Listening to his wife's peaceful breathing, he wondered what his next option was in relation to what had attacked him. However, his wondering thoughts were quickly interrupted by a shuffling outside the bedroom window.

Spinning his neck quickly towards the curtains

behind him, Stephen held his breath and waited for any further movement. After what seemed like an eternity, the strange sounds came once again from beyond the glass.

Raising himself upright on the mattress, Stephen stared at the moonlit curtains and suddenly he saw the silhouette of a figure scurrying away from the windowsill.

The startled man pulled his aching body from the warm bed, careful not to disturb his wife, and slowly stepped over to the heavy curtains draped over his bedroom window. Once he reached the window, he stood momentarily, listening attentively for any movement from beyond the glass.

Fearing the creatures had followed him home, Stephen slowly placed an unsteady hand on the curtain and gently pulled the cloth aside to reveal a tiny peephole.

He took a step forward and stared out into the darkness. It was a peaceful night and the bright moonlight helped him examine the area easier. His breathing deepened while he waited for any sign his property was being invaded.

Suddenly Stephen's eyes widened in terror. Standing to his right, lurking within the shadows was a small motionless figure, he then saw those pale eyes staring at him once again. His attention was drawn to further abominations advancing on his house.

"Stephen?" Louise called, from the comfort of their bed.

He turned to her shuffling about within the sheets, and quickly spun back to the glass to see that the fairies were gone.

"Is everything okay?" Louise continued, as she sat up.

"Yeah everything is fine love, just making sure the window was closed that is all," he said, not wanting to cause her any distress, even though his heart was beating rapidly.

"Come on, get back into bed, its freezing," his wife said, as she spun to her left side beneath the sheets.

"I'm just going to check on the boys. I'll be back in a second," he replied, in a rattling voice.

"What's wrong?" Louise quickly replied, shooting up on the mattress once again and switching on the bedside lamp.

"Nothing, I just couldn't sleep."

"Well you're acting strange. The kids are fine, come back to bed, you need to rest your leg," the concerned woman instructed.

"Okay I'm just going to go to the bathroom. I'll be back in a second," Stephen said, noticing his wife's growing worry due to his behaviour. He didn't want to tell her what he had just seen because first of all he thought she wouldn't believe him and second of all if she did, the torment of waiting for them to break into the house would be unbearable for the family, so he decided to manage it on his own.

Using the need to go to the toilet as an excuse, Stephen left the room, stepped through the sitting room, switched on the bathroom light, and closed the door. As quickly as he could, he checked his son's room to make sure they were safe and the windows were fully secured. Stephen, as hastily as his injured leg could carry him, checked both doors and all the windows once again to ensure they were closed and locked.

Glancing to the moon splashed kitchen window, Stephen couldn't help but feel as though they were playing with him on some sadistic level.

"You kept your time," Louise said, once he opened the bathroom door, flushed the toilet, washed his hands, and switched off the bathroom light. His wife not taking any notice of the odd sequence he carried out.

"Sorry," was all he could say, while he lowered himself onto the bed.

"Are you sure you're okay?" his wife said turning to him.

"Yeah, I just can't sleep that's all. Sorry I didn't mean to wake you," Stephen replied, his mind still on the creatures which were causing his anguish.

"Well you need to try, it's not going to do you any good walking around on that leg," Louise instructed, resting her head on his chest.

Stephen didn't sleep for the remainder of the night. He lay on his back, with his right arm around his beautiful Louise, staring towards the ceiling trying to rationalise what was happening to him and what lived in the fields around his house. His heartbeat raced and eyes quickly searched the darkness each time he heard a subtle creak throughout the house. Although he wanted to check the source every time, he didn't want to raise Louise's concerns any further.

When daylight showed itself on the bedroom curtains, Stephen turned to check on Louise, seeing she was still sound asleep, he climbed from the bed and walked over to the window.

Peering out through the glass, he looked for any evidence that the property had been invaded the previous night. Still slightly dark outside, he was greeted with a heavy mist which made it difficult to see any great distance, however from what he could tell, all looked normal and undisturbed.

Stephen then made his way towards his boy's bedroom, yawning deeply as he did. The combination of tiredness and pain bombarded him as he gently opened the bedroom door to check on his sons. Pushing open the door, he was welcomed by sounds of peaceful sleeping breaths as the heavy curtains helped keep the room shrouded in blackness. Before he closed the door, his attention was drawn to the right-hand side of the bedroom, eyes adjusting, his mouth widened as he spotted a small figure standing a few inches from his children.

Although he couldn't see it clearly, he could see the long strands of hair, extremely long, thin arms and those pale white eyes which were fixed on him.

Wanting to protect his children, Stephen stepped back into the room which triggered a forward movement from the fairy.

This caused Stephen to halt as he looked at the creature, which was now more visible. Its hideous face turned towards John and Owen's beds, and then back to Stephen before displaying a sinister, sharp, crack toothed grin. The creature casually stepped back into the dark area of the bedroom and disappeared before the horrified man's eyes.

Stephen moved as quickly as he could over to the corner, and moved the clutter of toys out of the way to reveal nothing. No sign of the evil creature and no indication of how it got in or out of the room.

"Morning Daddy," John said, as he rubbed his eyes to life in the bed.

Stephen pressed a hand against the cold wall, still shocked with what he had just witnessed.

"Daddy?" John called once again.

"Oh hey, how are you little fella?" he finally replied, as he turned to his son who was by then sitting up in his bed.

"You looking for something?" the young boy asked, wondering why his father was in the bedroom so early in the morning.

"No, just tidying up. We need to keep this place in order don't we," came the abrupt answer, the quickest one Stephen could create rather than explaining the truth.

He double checked the window to find it was still closed. How the hell did it get in here? Stephen thought to himself as he spun his eyes around the darkened room, however he knew looking for a rational explanation would yield no answer judging on what he had witnessed and the other events that had occurred recently. He considered momentarily that his mind was losing its grip on reality, but the injuries on his leg clarified that something sinister was descending on the family.

"Get some rest, you'll be getting up for school soon," Stephen instructed, leaving the room to check around the rest of the house.

The voice in his head screamed to him to tell his family to pack their bags and leave straight away, but he wondered what good it would do. Also what way would it look to his pregnant wife and their children if he started raving about evil fairies attacking him and breaking into the house. Plus, it seemed the creatures could now come and go as they pleased, so what would stop them from following him.

Stephen pulled the kitchen curtains aside and peered out into the morning once again, not knowing his neighbour had been brutally murdered, and his cold body was lying in the field beside the property.

By then the crows had started feasting on the elderly man's torn body. The eyes had been plucked from Sean's head and the crows had begun to pick at the loose flesh surrounding the dead man's wounds. As more and more scavengers joined the human carvery, the body was attacked from all directions.

"You're up very early, you sure everything is okay?" Louise asked, stepping into the kitchen behind her husband, knowing he should be resting.

"Everything is fine, I just couldn't get comfortable at all with my leg," Stephen said, turning to the beautiful woman behind him.

"Well go and sit down, that leg isn't going to get better at all if you keep moving around on it. There is no point in us going back to bed now, I'll get breakfast ready," Louise said, walking over to the fridge.

Stephen knew there was no point arguing with her and even if he did, it may raise even more suspicion, so he did as he was told and retreated into the sitting room and switched on the television.

Following breakfast, the children went to school and Louise decided to go out to get some groceries. Stephen offered to accompany her, but she was firm in her instruction for him to stay at home and rest.

Louise steered the car right and drove towards town. By then the mist had cleared somewhat as she glanced towards the fairy ring in the distance, where she had witnessed an unsettling experience, however, she put it down to tiredness and her mind playing tricks on her. Squinting her eyes, she spotted the large flock of birds circling, landing, and flapping about close to the circular landmark in the distance. Slowing the car, she thought, that was strange.

Chapter 6

Several days had passed without incident, however Stephen remained on edge. He tried to conceal his fear as best as possible, even though every sound within the house, every time the children or Louise went silent or every time the wind would cause the curtains to move, he was convinced the evil creatures were attacking.

Unknown to the rest of the community, Sean's body remained lying face down, being further mauled by the wildlife each passing day. Sean had no family left alive, and rarely would anyone visit him which made it exceedingly difficult for anyone to notice he was missing and dead.

"You seem to be moving a lot better on that now," Louise said to Stephen as he walked into the kitchen.

"Yeah it's healing nicely. I should be able to go back to work next week," Stephen replied, sitting at the table.

"I think the doctor should decide that! He only removed the stitches yesterday and reminded you that you need a little more time before returning to work," his wife instructed, turning to him and placing a plate of succulent rashers, sausages, pudding, and eggs with a helping of toast in front of him. The smell was enough to make his mouth water. "Those birds haven't left up there for the last couple of days," Louise continued, as she turned back to pour herself a warm cup of tea.

Outside, the countless birds were still feasting on Sean's corpse, some fought for position and others circled over the remains waiting for an opportunity to swoop in and pick a piece of cold flesh off for themselves.

"What are you up to today?" Stephen asked, paying no attention to his wife's observation.

"I'm going to go into town to pick up some things and no, before you ask, you're not coming with me," she smiled towards him as she joined him at the table.

"I haven't lost my leg you know," Stephen grinned before placing a sliced piece of pudding into his mouth.

"I know but rest up as much as possible. The more you rest the quicker you can get back to work." Words she knew would appeal to the workaholic.

Stephen rolled his eyes in response. By that stage, although he wouldn't admit it, he was reluctant to go back to his normal routine. He wondered what would happen if he left Louise in the house on her own during the day. Is that what they are waiting for, to attack when she is alone? He thought to himself a number of times over the previous days.

"Maybe you should invite Dan and Katie over this weekend? They've only been here once since we've moved in," Louise quickly suggested.

Dan was Stephen's older brother by three years

who owned and managed a small pub in Dublin. He married Katie when they were both young and had one teenage son.

Thinking to himself it might help take his mind off things having his brother over, Stephen nodded in agreement and said, "You know, that's actually not a bad idea. I'll ring him when you're out."

The brothers were always close and even though Stephen decided to move from the city, they often texted and spoke on the phone. When in each other's company, they would always be joking and teasing whoever was in the same room as them and in Stephen's opinion it may be just what he needed to help ease the strain building within him.

"Do you want me to pick you up anything when I'm out?"

"No thanks, I'm fine," Stephen said, as he scratched the top of the fresh bandage around his leg.

"Okay, well I'll be back as soon as I can," Louise said, standing from her chair. She kissed her husband on the cheek, collected the car keys, and left the house.

A silence fell around the tormented man sitting alone in the house. Looking down at the meal, he placed the knife and fork upon it, and slid it away from him. Eating was the last thing he wanted to do, he was just acting as normal as possible in front of his family. Picking up the warm cup of tea, he stood to his feet and stepped over to the kitchen sink. He again noted he was moving a lot better than he had been previously.

Pouring the tea down the sink, he too looked out into the distance and spotted the unusually large amount of birds flapping about, just a short distance from the fairy ring. Dread instantly crashed upon him as he wondered what was causing the animals to behave in such a way. He decided there was only one way to find out, even though he was terrified, he wanted to see what they were up to. Reaching into the drawer, Stephen retrieved a knife. He stepped over to the kitchen door and pulled on his work boots.

His paternal instinct was taking over, he wanted to ensure his family was safe and in no danger, so if this meant he had to conquer his fear and brave what was lurking in those fields once more in order to protect the ones he loved, he was prepared to do it.

Locking the door behind him, Stephen could hear the faint caws of the birds in the distance. When he turned to look in their direction, more winged creatures seemed to have joined the flock.

Walking to the front gate, on steadier feet than he had had over the last number of days, he looked left to ensure Mary was not out in her garden. Although she was a nice neighbour, Stephen didn't want to explain why he was venturing off into the fields beside their houses. Seeing that the coast was clear, he opened the gate and made his way towards the field entrance as quickly as he could.

When he reached the large rusted gate, Stephen took a deep inhale as the flashbacks of his attack quickly sprinted to the forefront of his mind and the pain he endured when the beast clawed at his flesh. Ensuring the knife was still at his waist, Stephen slid the cold, frost ridden latch across and moved into the long grass. Closing the gate behind him, he began to make his way towards the frenzied birds in the distance.

After several minutes, Stephen took a firm hold of the knife in his hand when he was just a short distance from the mound dominating the landscape. He wasn't sure if the sharp blade would even affect the fiends which dwelled within the fort, however he was determined to defend himself anyway he could. Continuing forward, he turned his attention to what was causing the birds to act in such a way. Stephen could see something laying on the ground, but he couldn't identify exactly what it was from a distance and due to the amount of crazed birds around it.

Keeping a close eye on the fairy ring, he made his way towards the flock.

Following a short walk, Stephen's eyes widened so much he could physically feel them strain. Before him, only a few steps away, he witnessed a human hand being picked at by the beaked animals. His gag reflex was triggered as his nostrils were filled with the pungent smell of death carried along with the small breeze. He quickly glanced towards the ancient cluster of trees and bushes not far from his side to double check that nothing was running toward him.

He moved closer and it was at that moment, he

recognised the partial side view of Sean's head.

"Sean," Stephen exhaled.

Reaching his deceased neighbour, he had to physically beat some of the ravenous animals off his corpse. Looking down at the man's torture-ridden face and the ripped skin along Sean's throat, Stephen knew life had long left his neighbour's body.

With the birds still circling overhead and the old man's blood beneath his feet, Stephen turned towards the fairy ring which by then seemed to pulsate with an evil energy.

"WHAT DID YOU DO?" he roared towards the home of the fairies, not caring if anyone heard him.

He waited for some kind of recognition, but no obvious response came.

Stephen turned back towards Sean, as he looked down at the torn corpse, he had no doubt the fairies were responsible, and he was determined not to let any of his family end up in the same condition.

"Come on out, I know you're in there," he said, stepping towards the fairy ring, angered at the thought of a defenceless old man being killed and left in such a way.

Suddenly, the sky grew dull as the breeze increased around him. The birds overhead flapped their wings as fast as they could while they dispersed from the area in all directions, it was then Stephen eyed the combination of long haired, balding and hairless figures emerging from the heavy undergrowth.

Their sinister grins shooting towards him made

him second guess his decision to return to the area where he had been attacked. However, looking at their sharp, jagged teeth, he was determined to stand his ground for the sake of his family.

"Why?" Stephen asked, referring to the dead man a few feet away.

He disturbed us, just as you did Stephen. He had nothing to give us, but you do! A voice sounded in the man's mind as he watched more and more of the horrible fairies crawl from the mound.

"What do you mean?" Stephen asked, holding the knife as tightly as he could, waiting for any attack.

Give us one of your children or you will all die! Filled his head, however not one of their mouths were moving.

Fear returned to Stephen upon being given the ultimatum.

"Not a chance, you'll have to go through me first!" he said, raising the blade before him.

Do you really think you have a choice? If we wanted you dead, you would be already. Willingly give us a child or you will watch them beg you for help as we take each of their lives. The fairies projected into his mind as they began walking towards him.

"Stay back, I mean it," Stephen said, witnessing creatures that were only meant to be the thing of old wives' tales making their way towards him.

One group stopped just a few feet from the man as another small group rounded him and collected Sean's body. They reached out their long limbs and dug their claws into what was remaining of his flesh and began dragging him towards the fairy ring.

"You humans are so predictable, we knew if we left him there rotting you would have to come up to see what was going on sooner or later," One creature said stepping forward from the large group gathering in front of him.

"Get away from him," Stephen roared, as he moved towards the monsters which were dragging him away.

Stephen slashed at the slender creatures as viciously as possible. Wide lacerations opened on their pale skin, however no blood poured from them and the injuries Stephen was inflicting were having absolutely no effect on the fairies.

"Please?" the man said, placing his hands on Sean's cold body in an effort to prevent them dragging him away.

It did no good, they were too strong for him and he had to release Sean as they pulled him into the fairy ring.

"A child or you all die," the fairies whispered as they began to retreat into the dense undergrowth.

"You can't have any of my children, take me!" he quickly fired back at the countless creatures before him.

"It's not you we want. The only reason you are still alive is that you have something of interest. Give us what we want or your entire family dies!" the last of the beasts said, before disappearing back into the fairy ring.

Stephen stood in disbelief at what he had just witnessed. Glancing down to the bloodless blade, the perplexed man couldn't rationalise how the injuries he inflicted had no effect on the sadistic creatures who dwelled within the soil just a short distance away from him. However, the thing that really strained his mind was the ultimatum the fairies had given him.

There was absolutely no way he could in his wildest dreams even consider giving one of his boys to those foul creatures, but could he really protect his family from them after what he had just seen?

With his head spinning and the body gone, Stephen turned and began to make his way back down towards the field entrance.

As before, when he had encountered the fiends, Stephen peered back occasionally to ensure nothing was following him home.

Reaching the gate, he quickly exited the field and turned left towards home.

Stepping towards his house, Stephen noticed Mary standing in her garden looking in his direction.

"Hi Stephen, have you got five minutes?" she asked, as he reached his front gate.

"I'm a little busy at the moment, can it wait?" Stephen replied, trying to deflect Mary's question.

"No, it's important, please I won't keep you long," she replied looking at him with the glimpse of worry sculpted upon her face.

"Is everything okay?" Stephen asked, his mind

throwing every possible eventuality at him.

"Come inside and I'll explain everything," Mary said, as she walked down to her gate and opened it.

Stephen said no more and did as he was asked.

Stepping through the front door, the smell of home baking filled his nostrils.

"Would you like anything to drink?" Mary asked, as she closed the door behind him.

"No thanks, I have to get back over to the house soon. What's wrong?" Stephen replied, as he turned around to face her.

"Okay, I think we should sit down first though," The middle aged neighbour said, opening the sitting room door to her right and motioning him inside.

Making his way into the room, Stephen took in the large amount of old photographs displayed around the walls and the numerous small ornaments resting upon the mantelpiece. It reminded him of Sean's house. To his right sat a large sofa, which is where he decided to rest while Mary outlined why she was so insistent on him speaking with her.

She sat down across from him in the opposite chair and said, "I don't know how to begin to be totally honest."

"Don't worry, just tell me what's wrong, I'll do anything I can to help," Stephen said, his mind still on the events he had witnessed minutes before.

Mary took a few deep inhales as she shuffled about uneasy on the chair. Brushing a strand of her greying hair back behind her ear, she looked back towards

Stephen.

"You've seen them haven't you?"

"Who?" Stephen asked, swallowing the dry lump in his throat.

"The fairies out in that accursed field. I heard you out there a few minutes ago and judging by the look on your face when you walked over here, I know I'm not wrong. They did that to your leg right?" Mary continued.

"I don't know what you are talking about," Stephen snarled, as he stood to his feet.

"If you don't do what they ask, your whole family will suffer," Mary replied in a strong tone.

Hearing those words caused the man to calm slightly and ease back down onto the sofa.

"What are they?" he asked, after he gathered his thoughts.

"I don't know. Fairies, Fae, Little People. I just know they are real, evil, and live out there in those fields. You know they are real now too don't you?" Mary said, sitting forward in the chair. "What did they ask you to do?"

"They... they said I have to give them one of my children or we will all die," Stephen finally replied, placing his head in his hands.

"How did it all begin, did you disturb them in some way?" Mary queried.

"Yes, I went inside that ring out there," Stephen explained.

"Oh no," Mary said, sitting upright.

"What?"

"That's the worst thing you can do. You are not supposed to step into their realm or disturb them in any way. It brings the wrath of the so-called fairies upon you," Mary replied.

"Wait a minute, how do you know about them?" Stephen asked, eyebrows scrunched in confusion.

It took a moment for Mary to acknowledge the question, and following another deep inhale, she began to explain her experience with the evil beasts.

"Although quite beautiful now, the splendour of the countryside around the area in the summer is awe invoking. As you can probably tell, I enjoy gardening and I take great pride in my work. Anyway, some time ago, the most beautiful, ruby flowers you have ever seen grew from that wrath, a type I had never seen before. I decided I must have some, so I collected a number of them and brought them home," Mary's face grew sadder as she continued her story. "That night, whatever they are that live in those fields, broke into my house and told me I had stolen from them and I would pay dearly for my ignorance. They said I had to surrender my child to them or everyone I loved would die in the most horrific and painful ways possible. You see Stephen, if you are to believe in the legends, the fairies would steal a human baby and replace it with their own, a changeling, and the parents would have to raise the inhuman child, a sort of way of removing humans from the land around them if you will. However, these seem to take pleasure out of forcing the parents to hand the child over to them themselves, a way to cause even further pain I suppose."

"I can't believe this," Stephen said.

"Obviously, I couldn't give them my beautiful Claire, so I made a deal with them," Mary added, tears building in her eyes.

"A deal?" Stephan quizzed, praying this was all just a crazy nightmare.

"Yes, I told them I would give my next born child to them if they would leave us in peace, but I'm at the age where the chances of me even becoming pregnant are lower. Why do you think I have so many random men calling over when Claire is in school? I'm trying to get pregnant unknown to them," Mary said, exploding into torrents of tears. "I don't know how long I have, but time is running out. I can't let them take her Stephen, what am I going to do?"

"We have to get help," Stephen said, listening to the woman's anguish and currently living through his own.

"Who would listen to us, let alone believe what we were telling them? Would you have believed what I was telling you if you hadn't encountered them yourself?" Mary asked, wiping her tears with the back of her hand.

"So, what, we just have to do what they ask us? I can't do that," he replied.

"What choice do we have? There is nothing we can do to stop them. If you don't obey their commands, you will experience bad luck and then the people you love will start to die," Mary affirmed.

Looking towards the shaken woman opposite him, Stephen wondered if it was the fairies who had caused her husband's death. His thoughts steered towards the family who had lived in the house before he and his family had moved in, the death of their son, and how Mary told Louise how he was found out in the fields. Did they also stumble upon the malevolent creatures which lurked in that mound, did their son die because of it, and were they forced to move because of their torment? Furthermore did the boy die in that way because they didn't surrender him to the fairies and would the fairy curse follow them wherever they ventured?

"What are we going to do?" Stephen finally asked.

"What we're told!" Mary stated.

"I better get back, Louise will be home soon," Stephen replied, standing to his feet, thoughts strained even further.

"Okay, but please don't tell anyone about them, we don't want their infection spreading any further than us. If word got out, the place would be swarmed by tourists looking to see if the stories are true."

After saying goodbye, the injured man slowly hobbled back to his house analysing the information. He agreed with his neighbour on some level, they should keep startling realisation fairies exist and they aren't as innocent as they have been depicted in order to help protect others from facing the same ultimatum he and his neighbour had been given. However, he couldn't just sit back and allow them to destroy his family.

Stepping through his house, Stephen made his way to the kitchen, fetched himself a glass, and poured himself some water, which was a welcome refreshment to his dry throat.

Looking out at the fairy fort, silhouetted against the sky, the thought of dosing it in petrol and setting it alit crossed his mind, but then again would it even have any effect of them he pondered.

"I'm back dear," Louise said, walking through the front door, Stephen had closed only seconds before.

Placing the glass into the sink, he donned his best fake smile and turned to her.

"You weren't long, how was town?" Stephen asked, sitting down at the kitchen table.

"Hectic as always, did you get up to much when I was out?" His wife asked as she placed the shopping bags on the table and pulled the bobble to unleash her long, flowing hair.

"No, nothing really. Just rested up, do you want a hand with those?" he asked.

"No, no you stay where you are, we want you fit and healthy as soon as possible," she smiled.

"Knew you'd say that," Stephen smiled in return.

As before, he hated lying to his wife, but he felt he needed to until he figured out the next step to take.

Later that afternoon when the two boys returned home from school, the family had dinner together and then sat down to watch television.

"Okay, time for bed," Louise instructed the children after checking her watch.

Outside the heavy darkness had once again devoured the countryside, a darkness which was different from the city nights the family had been so used to. In the countryside, there was no street light glow to help fight back some of the progressing blackness as it crashed across the landscape.

John and Owen did as they were told, and both went to the bathroom to brush their teeth.

"You've been very quiet this evening, everything okay?" Louise asked Stephen.

"Oh, I'm fine, just a little tired that's all," Stephen replied, not revealing he had spent most of the evening worrying once again.

"You should go early yourself tonight. I'm just going to get these tucked in," she said, standing from the couch and following the children to their room.

Shortly afterwards, Stephen and Louise decided to call it a night themselves and the house descended into a peaceful silence. It didn't take long for Stephen to drift off to sleep due to his mind being exhausted.

It was just after 3am when John awoke in his bed to the sounds of scratching in the corner of the bedroom. The bright moonlight which had developed over the course of the night helped his eyes adjust quicker to the darkness.

Looking towards his younger brother's bed, he could see Owen was still in a peaceful slumber. The scratching suddenly stopped, causing John to quickly turn his attention back to the darkest corner of the room. His breathing deepened as he slowly surveyed the area which the sounds had been emitted from, and he glanced around the rest of the room.

"John," hissed a voice slowly from the pulsating blackness.

Spinning his head quickly back to the corner, the young boy froze in terror when he spotted the outline of a figure standing motionlessly, staring back at him.

"You'll be ours soon," creeped a voice across the room towards the child.

The figure began to walk forward and the darkness concealing it followed.

"Dad…" John roared, watching the intruder get closer and closer.

Suddenly, the figure darted across the remaining space between it and the bed, raised its abnormally long hand, and grabbed the boy by his wrist.

John cried for help as he was dragged from the bed, which instantly awoke his brother and his parents. Hearing their son's pleas, Stephen and Louise leaped from their bed and raced through the sitting room towards their son's bedroom.

Flicking on the light, Stephen spotted John in tears on the floor, Owen sitting up on his bed in shock.

Louise raced past Stephen to her petrified child.

"What's wrong? What happened?" she asked, as she took the child in her arms to try and comfort him.

"There is something in here, it grabbed me," John

spluttered.

Both Stephen and Louise examined the room, but nothing could be seen. Stephen checked the wardrobe and underneath each of the boy's beds.

"There is nothing in here," Stephen confirmed, however he knew he didn't have to think too hard to identify what was behind the attack.

"There is, there is a person in here. He said my name, and then pulled me from my bed," John cried into his mother's shoulder.

Louise looked towards her husband with a concerned look whilst she continued to slowly rub the back of her son's head.

"It must have been a bad nightmare pet, everything is ok now," she said, as she turned towards Owen, whose face was twinkling with tears, having witnessed the unsettling event.

"Come on guys, you can sleep in our room tonight," Stephen said, as he stood aside, holding the bedroom door open.

Louise helped John to his feet and held out her hand towards Owen.

"I'll be in in a second," Stephen said to Louise as she stepped out into the hall, and made her way back towards her bedroom.

"There was someone in there Mammy," Stephen heard John reconfirm as they moved through the sitting room.

Turning back towards the boy's beds, Stephen searched the room again and as before, nothing out of the ordinary could be found. However, the fear he had experienced first-hand due to those horrid beasts living out in that field, was nothing compared to the anguish knowing his family was being randomly attacked.

Following the quick search, Stephen pulled back the curtains and stared out into the night, looking in the direction of the dreaded fairy ring. He wanted nothing more in the world to march up there at that exact moment and kill each and every one of the creatures who dwelled within the mound, but he knew he did not have the means to even injure them.

Stephen switched off the boy's bedroom light, checked the front door handle, and returned to his own bedroom.

"What did it look like?" Stephen asked his son.

"Really?" Louise said, before the boy could answer.

"What? I just want to know, what's wrong with that?" Stephen uncharacteristically snarled back. The event was beginning to weigh heavy on his mind.

"I couldn't really see it, but it tried to drag me away," John replied, whilst his mother continued to cradle the boy in her arms while shooting a disapproving stare towards her husband.

"I'll be back in a second," Stephen said.

He left his family and went to check on the back door to the house, to ensure it was still secure.

Stepping into the small kitchen, the bright moonlight shone against the curtains pulled across the window before him. Again, he could see nothing in the darkness. As he reached out to check on the handle, Stephen's attention was drawn to the flat roof above his head. Standing as silently as he could within the shadow splattered room, he looked towards the ceiling, and listened to what seemed to be footsteps above his head.

Frustrated with the mind games he was being subjected to, Stephen flicked on the kitchen light, quickly spun the key, pushed down on the door handle, and stepped out into the cold night.

Paralysed in place, he listened as the sound of footsteps made their way along the flat kitchen roof towards him. Keeping his gaze fixed on the edge of the roof above him, his eyes widened when one of the hideous creatures revealed itself.

Stephen took a number of steps backwards as the fairy's mouth widened to a sinister smile. The creature stepped forward to the edge of the roof, kneeled, reached its extremely long limbs out before it, and placed its claws into the tiny crevasses in the wall. The man watched in disbelief as the fairy crawled down the wall headfirst. Reaching the ground, the fiend crawled another few feet, and stood upright.

"Please just leave us alone. I'm sorry, I didn't mean to disturb you," Stephen said, as he stood alone in the night, fearing the fairy would lunge at him any moment and rip him to pieces.

Standing in front of him, he once again studied the unsettling sight, the most significant attributes were the arms which reached down to just below its bandy knee, the sixth toe half way up the fairy's feet, and no nose displayed upon the beast's face.

The pure white eyes glaring at him, caused Stephen to apologise once again and it was then the grinning lips parted, displaying jagged teeth as the creature spoke to him.

"Your apologies mean nothing to us. Give us what we want or we will take them all from you," the fairy said, in a hoarse tone.

"You were in my boy's room weren't you? Leave them alone and take me, I'll do anything you want but leave my family in peace," Stephen pleaded, ensuring not to raise his voice to alarm Louise and the children inside.

"Do you really think you can bargain with us? We could take every one of your pathetic species in an instant and you could do nothing about it, only scream for your life. However, where is the fun in that, where is the pure suffering in that? No we want you to willingly give us one of your children as we watch your heart shatter to pieces, but if you don't we will take everyone you love before we take your life," the beast smirked.

"Please just take me, I'm the one who disturbed you, surely I'm the only one who should be punished," Stephen said, knowing it would fall on deaf ears.

"We already have you, give us what we want or you will suffer torture unlike anything you have experienced before in your miserable life,"

"Why are you doing this?" the defeated man sighed.

"Because we can," the fairy said, mouth widening further with a smile.

"You'll never get away with this, with what you're doing to Mary and with what you did to Sean," Stephen stated as confident as he could.

"Fool, you really have no idea what we are capable of. No one can help you, no one can stop us. Give us what we want or you will experience pain like you never have before!" The creature said, before disappearing into the darkness.

Realising he needed to return to his shaken family, Stephen quickly stepped back into the kitchen, shut the door behind him and locked it.

Thankfully, he had closed the sitting room door when he had moved through the house, so he was hopeful that Louise nor the children had heard his conversation with the mythical creature outside his house.

When he reached the bedroom, John had calmed down in his mother's arms, Owen was falling in and out of slumber.

"Everything okay?" Louise whispered.

"Yeah, I just wanted to check around the house. It must have been a dream," Stephen said, agreeing with his wife's initial thought on John's experience.

Staring into his wife's beautiful brown eyes, he wanted nothing more than to tell her everything which had been going on over the last number of days, however he thought by then things had gone too far and if he did confide in her, the evil creatures would take out their vengeance on her.

Looking towards her husband, Louise noticed something different about him, she noted a change in his behaviour and she couldn't quite identify the cause. However, she put it down to his recent injury and his frustration due to not being able to work or continue renovating their small country cottage.

Neither Stephen nor Louise knew their partner had encountered the evil which dwelled out in the countryside, Stephen more so.

"Okay, well come to bed, it's late," Louise instructed, as she reached across the bed and pulled the large, puffy duvet to one side.

Stephen switched off the light and made his way over to the bed, the bright moonlight aiding his journey.

He lowered himself slowly onto the mattress and looked left towards his family, Owen and John lying between him and Louise. He said goodnight to his wife, however, he kept looking in her direction. His family was his entire world and there was no way he was going to let them be harmed in any way once air still entered his body.

Stephen was determined to do everything in his power to protect his children and pregnant wife, he just needed to figure out how he was going to do it.

Chapter 7

Stephen awoke the following morning to the sounds of his children's laughter, a sound which instantly brought a huge smile to his face and filled him with joy. The nice feelings were quickly crushed by the cascading flashbacks of the night before, and the ultimatum he was faced with at the hands of those small, slender, long limbed, jagged haired and bald beings.

"Quiet children, Dad is still sleeping," Stephen heard Louise say softly in the sitting room, as the volume of the early morning cartoons was lowered on the television.

Tears saturated his eyes and the corners of his mouth arched downwards as the thought of life without them tormented his mind. The sudden image of a bloodied John being dragged into the fairy ring, crying for his life plagued his thoughts.

Stephen released a low whimper, drying his eyes with the back of his hands.

He was being slowly broken down and he thought to himself time must be surely running out before more drastic measures were taken against him. He lay in bed contemplating and arranging his thoughts, trying unsuccessfully to lower the severity of the situation, however no matter how many ways he played the scenario out in his head, he still lost.

His attention turned to the silence echoing through the house. How long had he been daydreaming, he thought to himself as he rubbed his drowsy eyes again.

The exhausted man pulled himself upright on the mattress and stood to his feet. Thankfully, his leg felt a lot better with each passing day and that morning was no different.

After getting dressed, he walked into the empty sitting room and looked towards the clock. His panic was averted somewhat eyeing that it was just after 9am which indicated the children would be in school and Louise had possibly gone into town again as she did most mornings once she had cleaned around the house.

Stephen made his way to the kitchen, retrieved a glass from the cupboard, and poured himself some water, one of the first things he noticed when he moved from the city was the cooler, fresher tasting water from the tap.

Dread filled him once more eyeing the fairy mound in the distance, hugged by the early morning fog.

Just as his mind was about to run riot, as he gulped down the cold liquid, Stephen heard the front door unlock and footsteps make their way through the sitting room towards him. Holding the glass tightly, he readied himself to use it as a weapon just in case the evil monstrosities had decided to break into his house again.

Stephen spun quickly, ready to fling the glass at an intruder, however, he was relieved to see his beautiful wife walking towards him.

"I saw your friend," Louise said, as she stepped over to the table, placing a single bag upon it.

"My friend?" Stephen queried, as he placed the glass safely into the sink and turned back to her.

"Yeah Sean was standing at the end of his driveway on my way back here just now. I pulled over and we had a quick chat. He's a lovely man isn't he?" Louise said, as she took some packaged meat from the bag and placed it into the fridge.

Stephen stared at her in shock as she closed the fridge door. He was convinced he had misheard her, knowing Sean had long left this world.

"Sean? Are you sure?" he asked, his eyebrows unable to scrunch down his face any further.

"What?" Louise asked, as she turned to him smiling. "Yeah, plump man, grey hair, lives in the farmhouse just up the road. Are you feeling okay?" she said in a sarcastic tone, placing the back of her hand to his forehead.

"Yeah... yeah of course," Stephen replied, as a numb feeling began to slowly make its way through his body. "What did he say?"

"Oh, not much, just the usual chit chat," Louise smiled as she flicked on the kettle.

Stephen kept his composure as much as he could as he stepped into the sitting room and lowered himself into a chair.

What the hell is going on? I saw his body! I saw them drag the corpse away in front of me! He thought to himself as he bit down hard on the fingernails on his right hand trying to contemplate what he had been told.

There was only one way to ease the newly added torment to his mind, he would have to go to the farmhouse and see for himself, see if indeed a man had returned from the dead.

Stephen stood from the comfortable chair and fetched his coat.

"I'm just going to stretch this out a little," he said, referring to his recovering injury, as he pulled the coat around his shoulders.

"Are you sure that's a good idea?" Louise asked in a concerned manner, as she joined him in the sitting room.

"Oh yeah, I'm feeling a lot better and I'm only going for a little walk. Nothing too strenuous I promise," he said, leaning over and kissing her on her soft, warm cheek.

"Okay, well I suppose you need to get out sooner or later, I can imagine being stuck indoors is driving you crazy. Just be careful and take your time!" Louise instructed.

Stepping outside, the gentle wisp of country air caressed his face, which in turn made Stephen pull the collar of the jacket up tightly around his neck as he began to make his way down the driveway towards the gate.

He looked to his left in the direction of Mary's and cast his mind to the torment she was also enduring at the hands of the evil, little beasts. However, his main concern now was what his wife had just told him. Had she really spoken to Sean, and if so, how was it possible? He calculated over and over again in his mind, trying to find the correct answer.

Moving along the small country road towards Sean's farmhouse, Stephen stepped past the field where the fairies dwelled as quickly as his legs could carry him.

There is no way she saw him, it's just not possible! Before he knew where the time had gone, Stephen rounded the corner, just before the driveway which led up to Sean's house, a house which should be empty based on what the fairies had done to the elderly farmer who once occupied it. He thought of telling the police about the incident in the field and what they had done to Sean, but to Stephen the evidence was gone, and he didn't want to taunt their evil anger any further.

Stephen paused at the gate momentarily, rationalising his wife must have spoken with someone other than who she had claimed to be Sean.

Knowing there was only one way he was going to be sure, Stephen took a deep inhale and began to make his way up the old, dirt, driveway.

As he moved closer to the house, Stephen reminded himself to glance left and right along the way to ensure there were none of those hideous creatures lurking in the hedging, waiting to ambush him once he was some distance from the road. He turned his attention back to the old farmhouse in front of him, a building which was eerily quiet. However, he was somewhat relieved as the noiseless house meant that so far, his original thoughts were correct, Sean was dead and gone.

Stephen's eyes turned to the windows of the house and all he could detect behind the glass was obscure blackness. Reaching the house, he moved to the sitting room window and peered inside.

Everything looked normal and was in the same condition as the day he left the house. Again, the thing that popped back into his mind was his wife had spoken to someone else and not Sean himself. Before he moved his face back from the window, he glimpsed something move in the corner of his eye, however when he spun his head towards it, nothing could be seen.

Undeterred, Stephen made his way to the front door. Thinking that knocking wouldn't be appropriate, he tried the handle and to his surprise it turned freely downwards, and he slowly pushed it open. Leaning left and right, Stephen viewed the interior as much as possible before he was going to commit to stepping inside.

Eyeing nothing lurking in the immediate vicinity, the Stephen slowly moved in through the doorway, while remaining on high alert for any advancement or noise not generated by himself.

In any other situation, the first thing he would have done after opening the door would be to shout, "Hello," but he refrained from doing so, in order to keep his visit as discreet as he possibly could.

He walked to the sitting room and there was no sign of Sean's reanimated corpse.

Deciding to investigate the rest of the house, Stephen turned, and it was at that specific moment his mouth and eyes widened and his heart raced faster and faster.

Above him, clung to the corner of the high ceiling, was Sean, who had been studying Stephen's every move since he had entered the room.

"Sean?" Squeezed its way past Stephen's quivering lips after a moment's silence which felt like an eternity.

No response came from the man glaring down towards him, his fingernails dug deep into the hard wall.

"But I saw your body, you were dead," Stephen continued in horror, as he began to back away slowly from his until now, recently dead neighbour.

Sean kept his gaze upon Stephen, not blinking even for a moment. Suddenly, Sean's face started contorting rapidly in unhuman ways, and he began grinning wider with each passing second. Without warning, he released his grip, fell to the floor, and landed on his feet in front of the awestricken man.

"You're one of them aren't you?" Stephen

stuttered as he stepped further away from the thing in front of him, knowing that no one, especially a man of Sean's age could do what he had just witnessed.

The fiend in the guise of Sean, lunged forward and grabbed Stephen firmly by his neck.

Stephen's fight instinct immediately kicked in and he began to punch his assailant in the head as hard as possible, however no matter how hard he threw his fist, it seemed to have absolutely no effect on the thing which began to slowly squeeze his throat.

"What are you?" Stephen asked, trying to catch his breath whilst he grabbed the wrist at his neck with his tired hand.

"Who do I look like?" slithered from the mouth before him, followed by another large smile.

"You're not Sean, you're from out there aren't you!" Stephen quickly replied, his body straining further with each passing second.

"Well, aren't you a smart one. Yes, you're right, I am. We can't have people randomly disappearing without nothing to take their place can we? It would just draw too much attention to us. Anyway, now that I have taken on this pathetic fool's identity, who is going to believe you about what we did to him?" the fairy replied in Sean's voice.

"Why are you doing this?"

"Because we hate your species and because we can," was the answer given to Stephen's question.

"You'll never get away with it," Stephen said, as he placed his other hand on the arm restraining him.

"Oh yeah?" the fairy disguised as a human said, as it pulled him closer. "What are you going to do about it?" and then he applied more pressure upon the man's neck.

The beast mockingly awaited a response, but all that came from Stephen's mouth were the gulping sounds of him choking.

"You've no idea how many of us are out there in your world. How would you know, you could walk by one of us in broad daylight and you would just assume it's another filthy human. Now don't ever come back up here again or you won't be leaving, don't you have something to do for us?" The fairy smiled, referring to the ultimatum of handing up a child.

"I'll never give you one of my boys," Stephen confirmed, anger building in him due to the thought of any harm coming to his children.

"Give one of them willingly to us or they will all die as you watch them helplessly," the fairy threatened, the foul stench of its breath crashing against Stephen's face.

"Your wife seems really nice, it would be a terrible shame if we had to rip her to pieces in front of her offspring and lover. Give us a child or we will tear your family apart," the fiend said, glaring at Stephen, as it began to walk towards the front door.

There was so much pressure on Stephen's neck at that stage, he couldn't get any further words past his lips.

Face reddening, the monstrosity held Stephen to one side, opened the door and tossed him outside.

"Go on, leave while you still have your legs to carry you." the fairy said, slamming the door.

Disorientated, Stephen lifted himself to unsteady feet and paused momentarily, staring at the old, farmhouse door.

He knew fairies and the like should only be the stuff of old wives' tales, however he was caught up in their sinister plans, plans which had the goal of tearing his family apart.

Stephen rubbed his neck in an attempt to ease the pain, which was slowly pulsating its way through him. Realising there was nothing more he could do, he left for home.

As he walked along the quiet country road, he felt helpless. Who in their right mind would believe what he was going through, and furthermore, was there anything he could do to stop the fiends which were praying on him?

"So how was your walk?" Louise asked, hearing the front door opening.

"Yeah good, thanks," Stephen replied, as he slumped down onto the sitting room couch, his head straining with stress.

For the remainder of the day Stephen spent most of his time alone, trying to figure out what would be the best solution to the situation he found himself. Also was there anyone out there that he could confide in? He knew he couldn't tell his wife about the recent events as he didn't want to cause her any upset or fear.

Meanwhile Mary, said goodbye to another man who had visited her house for sexual pleasure, little did any of the men who called to her home know she was actually the one using them.

She always ensured the strangers who entered her home were gone by the time her daughter was back from school. Mary had always prided herself on being a good mother and would do absolutely anything to protect her beloved Claire.

As always, when Claire arrived home from school, Mary had their dinner ready on the table so they both could sit down and have it together. Afterwards, she helped her child with her homework and then both would watch the daily television soaps together.

Mary glanced to the clock later that night, the hands read 11:35pm as the coal in the open fire began to cool to a dull red. She stood from the comfortable armchair and walked over to the television. She flicked off the power button, and placed the fireguard in front of the dying flames. She made her way over to the sitting room window and pulled back the curtain to ensure the handle was firmly closed. While doing so, aided by the bright moonlight, Mary noticed the thick, swirling fog building outside with every passing second.

She returned the curtain to its original position and continued through the house ensuring everything was secure.

What Mary failed to notice lurking within the fog was the growing number of small, dark figures surrounding her house.

Mary had only been asleep for about an hour until her slumber was interrupted by sounds in the hallway outside her bedroom door.

Puzzled, she threw the heavy duvet from her body to one side, flicked on the bedside light, and climbed to her feet, listening to what sounded like numerous feet making their way along the wooden floor just beyond the closed door.

Her mind instantly shot towards the malevolent creatures who dwelled a short distance from her home.

Thinking of Claire's safety, Mary quickly placed her hand upon the door handle, pushed it down and opened the door slightly. Although she would do anything to protect Claire from harm, fear still had a restraint on her.

The light from Mary's bedroom cut its way out into the hallway like a thin blade along the floor, as she peered out towards her daughter's room. The movements around the house had ceased as she concentrated on the darkness, awaiting any obvious movements within it.

Taking a deep inhale, thinking of the unlimited evil associated with the monsters that lived out in the fields, Mary swung open the door and raced towards

Claire's room.

Mary pushed open her daughter's bedroom door to see the window open and curtains pulled aside, terror instantly crashed over her. She didn't need to turn on the bedroom light due to the bright moonlight beating its way into the room, to see that Claire's bed was empty.

She raced to the window just in time to witness Claire being dragged away into the darkness by countless fiends, one of the fairies was covering her mouth so she couldn't scream for help.

Witnessing the sheer fear and hopelessness in her daughter's eyes as she was taken from her home by creatures who were only meant to exist in old Irish tales, Mary climbed to the window, when, "Mary," hissed a voice slowly from behind her.

Turning and placing herself firmly back onto the floor, Mary eyed numerous fairies standing in the room with her.

"Please, I'm trying my best for you, please give me some more time, I'll provide a child for you just give Claire back to me," Mary begged, knowing with each passing second, her daughter was being taken further and further away from her.

"Too late, you had your chance, we told you to give us your child willingly or we would take her," one of the beasts declared, as they started walking towards the helpless woman.

"I tried to get pregnant, but it just didn't happen, please don't do this," was Mary's plea as she backed herself tightly up against the wall.

One of the fairies stepped out from the group, holding something wrapped in tattered rags. The slender creature placed the item at Mary's feet, then looked up towards her with its white eyes, grinned at her, and moved away.

Mary was paralysed with terror whilst the fog outside began to slowly weave its way into the room around her. She looked down towards the object which had been placed in front of her as it began to move about on the floor.

Her eyes widened in shock as she witnessed a tiny arm covered in a strange transparent goo, sprout from the bundle of cloth.

The group of fairies moved forward and gathered around the abomination developing on the floor at the horrified woman's feet.

Next, grew two legs and the creature stood to its feet. Another arm burst from the tattered cloth and pulled the rag away to reveal the face on an infant, however not a normal baby. This monstrosity had pure white eyes and sharp teeth just like the other fairies.

The beast looked towards Mary and released an inhuman roar and it began to convulse in front of her.

The creature began to grow, as blonde hair sprouted from its head. Mary looked on as the thing in front of her began to take on some very recognisable features. The fairy's face stretched slightly, its eyes developed a blue colour, and before she could rationalise what was happening, Mary was looking at her daughter standing in old, dirty rags before her.

"What is this?" she asked, shivering in terror.

"It's your daughter. Now it's time," a voice whispered through the darkness.

"Please give me back my daughter, I just need a little more time," Mary appealed to the group moving towards her.

Her cloned daughter stood in place as the rest of the creatures moved past her towards the helpless woman.

Mary realised the time for talking was over and tried to make her escape through the window her beloved Claire had been dragged from.

Her attempt was in vain however as the fairies quickly swarmed upon her, dug their claws deep into her flesh, and dragged her back into the dark room.

Feeling the warm blood flow from her wounds to the floor, she was forced face down upon, the middle-aged woman began to scream for her life. The fiends then dragged her further into the house and one of them placed a jagged claw over her mouth in order to dull her cries for help.

The beasts forced her to sit in one of the chairs in the sitting room as others began to claw viciously at her legs through the thin, white night dress she was wearing.

Agonising mummers and trashing about in the chair was the only thing Mary could do in response.

One of the fairies placed its long fingers through her hair and pulled her head to one side, as the others kept removing chunks of skin and muscle from the defenceless woman.

"You should have just handed her over, we always get what we want," the beast said, in relation to Claire.

The fairy sliced at Mary's face countless times until life left her. Once they were finished, the skin on the woman's face and body looked like bright red, damp wallpaper falling off a wall.

One of the creatures returned to Claire's room and from the darkness outside, was handed another bundle of rags through the window from another.

The fairy returned to the sitting room, placed the shapeshifter on the floor, which took on the form of the deceased woman. They cleaned the murder scene, collected the body, and carried it back with them to the fairy ring in the fields.

Mary, the true Mary, would never be seen again.

Chapter 8

The following morning came bright and warmer than usual, one of nature's little gifts at that time of year when the leaves have left the trees.

Calmness had instilled itself outside the two terrorised households as the small wildlife went about its daily business.

Inside, Stephen opened his aching, tired eyes. His whole body felt drained and fatigued, the complete opposite feeling of a good night's sleep. The sunlight had begun to invade the room as he turned to look at Louise still enjoying her Saturday morning lie on. The couple always looked forward to the weekend after a busy week, however Stephen's joy had been tarnished as of late.

He raised himself from the bed, swivelled and sat, feet touching the cold floor, momentarily with his hands clasped together, and hoped the fogginess would leave his head soon.

He stood and went to use the bathroom, trying his utmost to remain quiet. Stephen checked on the children, his eyes couldn't help veering to the corner where he had witnessed the figure in the room previously, thankfully nothing was lurking there.

Stephen returned to his bedroom, lay back down beside Louie, and stared at the ceiling above him.

Terrible thoughts began to seep uncontrollably into his mind. What if I did give them one of the boys, would that make them stop? Upsettingly pushed its way to the forefront of his reflection. He turned to his side and tried to concentrate on anything than what was bombarding him, but then, which one would I choose? He thought.

Stephen hated himself for thinking such things and the only thing he could visualise was the sadistic, evil, fanged grin towards him and pale eyes staring at him.

The fairies were the most disturbing things he had ever witnessed, and he couldn't stop thinking about them and what they required him to do so he and the remainder of his family could live in peace.

The early morning chirps of the birds became hypnotising and he found his heavy eyelids beginning to close under the weighing pressure.

Another hour or so passed before Louise climbed from the comfort of their bed. Seeing her husband in a sound slumber, Louise decided to allow Stephen to enjoy his rest.

She made her way to the kitchen first and pulled back the curtain to allow the beautiful sunshine to burst into the room around her. Louise lifted the kettle to check the water content, switched it on, and then retrieved an egg carton from the fridge. She placed it onto the table and returned to the sitting room in order to reveal the nice day outside.

Reaching for the curtains, she pulled them aside and instantly noticed, Mary, standing at the edge of the garden next door, staring towards the McKenna house.

Louise couldn't help but notice the huge grin on the Mary's face as she maintained her glare towards Louise and Stephen's home. Seconds later, Louise witnessed Claire, Mary's daughter step down through the dew-covered grass towards her mother, who still hadn't taken her eyes off the house.

Claire's movements were slow and robotic. When she reached Mary, she too turned to face Louise.

Uneasiness overcame the woman as the pair remained motionless, dead-eyed, wide grinned looking back towards her through the glass.

Her attention was drawn to the sounds of Owen and John's bedroom door opening, so she produced a polite wave towards the individuals surveying her home to help relieve the tension she was feeling. A few moments passed until Mary slowly raised her right hand upright and gave a sluggish, finger wave in return.

As the children came into the sitting room, she turned to them, "Morning you two, go brush your teeth and I'll get breakfast ready," she smiled to them, moving away from the window.

While the children were enjoying their boiled eggs and toast, Stephen awoke, still exhausted, pried himself upright on the mattress and got dressed. A constant tiredness had befallen him and no matter how much he tried to achieve any form of rest, it just was not possible.

As he made his way to the kitchen to his family, he glanced outside and saw Mary and her daughter still staring towards the house, however he didn't pay much attention to them.

"Uncle Dan is coming over later," Louise said to the children who both smiled from ear to ear hearing the news. "Morning love, can I get you anything?" she said to her husband as he sat down at the table.

"No, I'm fine thanks, I'll grab something in a bit. I see we have an audience outside!" he replied, referring to the usual behaviour of Mary and her daughter.

"They're still there? They were outside about an hour ago too," Louise stated.

"I'll go and see if everything is okay," Stephen said, finding it a little strange.

He stood from the table, slipped on his work boots, and made his way to the front door. He noticed his leg injury had almost fully healed, and pain was no longer an issue.

The refreshing country air immediately filled his nostrils when he opened the door. He turned and said good morning to Mary, who was still there with her daughter facing his home. There was no response.

"Everything okay?" he asked, ensuring the door was closed behind him.

Again, no response or recognition of his presence as the pair remained firmly in position, both still projecting their out of sorts smiles.

Confused, Stephen moved towards his neighbours to see what had a firm hold of their interest.

"Morning Mary, how are you?" he said reaching her.

Instantly he noticed their unblinking eyes had not moved from the direction of his home and their smiles looked painfully wide.

Uneasiness befell him as he wondered why the pair's expressions had not changed in any way.

"Is something wrong?" he asked.

"Oh Stephen, sorry, we didn't see you there," Mary sharply replied, as she turned to him and maintained the creepy smile.

Stephen briefly glanced towards Claire, who still hadn't regarded him.

Didn't she see me? He thought to himself in disbelief.

"So, what's going on?" he quizzed, referring to their odd behaviour.

"Oh, we were just admiring what you've done with the place. Isn't it amazing how quickly things can change around here?" Mary stated, as she momentarily turned back towards the house.

"Thanks, I thought there was something wrong," he replied.

"No, nothing is wrong, everything is as it should be," Mary answered.

Seconds later, Stephen noticed a huge, blue bottle fly land on Mary's face, then crawl its way to her left eye and pause at the side of the eyelid. It then made its way to her mouth and again remained there for a number of seconds before buzzing away.

Stephen thought it a little unusual as he rationalised a fly landing on a person's face would surely trigger an auto response in them to swipe it quickly away, however her smile never changed.

"Okay, well I suppose I better go back inside, busy day ahead," Stephen said, still baffled by their unusual behaviour.

"Why don't you send the children over to us, Claire would love someone to play with. Isn't that right Claire?" Mary said.

"Yes, it would be really fun," the statue-like child replied.

"No, not today I'm afraid, as I said we have a busy one ahead of us, thanks though," he responded.

"Are you sure? We don't mind lifting the burden for a while," Mary shot back and moved closer.

"Burden?" Stephen repeated, disgust fuelling his emotion.

"Ah you know what I mean, sometimes you just want to get rid of them wouldn't you agree?" Mary said, her smile by then turning to a serious glare. "Just send them over and we'll look after them for you."

The thought of erupting into a litany of insults, and who did she think she was speaking to him about his children in such a way, was bubbling inside him, however he decided to hold his outrage behind his teeth, turned, and walked away.

When Stephen reached the front door, he glanced back towards the pair who were still looking towards his house. He knew he had other things to be worrying about, so he decided to leave them there and stare to their hearts content.

"So, what did she say? What's wrong?" Louise asked, hearing the door close behind him.

"Nothing at all, everything is fine," Stephen said, sitting down in the sitting room.

"Well at least they are going back inside now. You must have a way with words eh?" she smiled as she turned back from the large sitting room window, and gave her husband a hug.

He smiled in response.

"I just got off the phone with Katie. She said they will be here around three this afternoon. Why don't you get a little rest before then," Louise said, and returned to the kitchen to continue working on the food preparation for them.

Stephen didn't need to be told twice and was happy to sit in comfort as he watched his beloved family go about their daily lives, oblivious to the torment he was being subjected to, and the danger he was trying to protect them from.

Stephen's brother, Dan and his wife Katie arrived later that afternoon.

The smell of home cooking instantly filled their nostrils as they stepped into the cottage, Katie with a bottle of wine in hand for their dinner later that evening.

"It really has turned out fantastic, it's a credit to you both," Dan said, referring to the house, as he kissed Louise on the cheek.

"And how is my little brother doing?" Dan said, wrapping an arm around him. "Leg is far better I see,"

"Yeah I should be back to work soon," Stephen said, trying as much as possible to hide the fact he was terrified to leave his family alone in or around the house.

"Brian decided not to come?" Louise asked, as they all moved into the sitting room and made themselves at home.

"Yeah, he is over at a friend's house until later. He is at that age now where he wants to hang out with his friends more than us," Katie replied.

The group laughed. Seconds later, Dan's nephews came into the room and raced over to their uncle and then to Katie, giving them each a hug.

"What are you feeding these guys, they are nearly as tall as me," Dan said, his face illuminated with joy.

For the next hour or so, Dan and Stephen stayed in the sitting room playing computer games with the children while Katie sat with Louise in the kitchen, helping with the food preparation as the cooking dictated. Of course, Louise told her not to be silly and sat down and relax, but Katie would have none of it and wanted to help with whatever she could.

"Oh that looks beautiful," Katie stated, referring to the home of the fairies in the middle of the field as the sunlight shone through the thick branches and bushes as it set behind it, creating a hypnotic scene.

"Yeah they call it a fairy ring apparently," Louise

said, joining her at the sink.

"A fairy ring?" Katie asked, as she turned to her.

"Yeah our neighbour was talking to me about it, it's an old rath of some sort, been there for countless years," Louise explained.

"I remember my father telling me about fairy rings when I was younger. People still have a huge superstition surrounding them to this day. Makes you wonder where all the stories and legends began wouldn't it," Katie said.

"Yeah, I was actually up there some time ago, stunning," Louise added.

"Oh, I hope you didn't disturb the fairies, they'll get you for that you know!" Katie said, playfully nudging Louise as the pair stared at the structure.

"I'll just send them after you instead," Louise giggled.

Dinner was served as the light faded to darkness outside the home. Afterwards, the children went to their room to watch television, Katie and Louise sat at the kitchen enjoying tea, while Stephen and his brother went to the sitting room with a couple of beers. Katie was the designated driver for the evening.

"God, Louise's cooking is unreal, I don't know if I can even fit this in," Dan grinned as he snapped open the top of the ice-cold beer can.

"Better not let Katie hear you say that," Stephen joked, as he too began to sip the cold liquid.

"Hey, when Katie cooks, she's the best and whenever I get free food, that cook is the best," Dan said, as the pair burst into laughter.

"So, what else has been going on? You've settled in great and it won't be long now until you have another baby in the house," Dan asked, as he took another mouthful of beer.

Stephen glanced out to his pregnant wife sitting across from Katie and joy filled him at the thought of them welcoming another child into the world, however this was quickly overcome with dread due to the hideous creatures who were hell bent on destroying what he loved so much. He couldn't let it happen and was determined to protect his family no matter the cost.

"Everything okay Steve?" Dan asked, noting his distant stare into the flames within the fireplace.

No response came as Stephen lost himself within the swaying blaze and the heat it was casting out into the room.

"Steve?" his brother called once again.

This snapped his attention back to the room he was sitting within. Stephen looked towards his older brother and then to his wife once more. He decided he needed to vent his torment to someone before his head imploded and knew he could confide in Dan no matter what. He stood to his feet and walked over to the door separating the sitting room and kitchen. He smiled to Louise and closed it over.

"There must be a game on the television," Louise smiled to Katie, and they continued with their conversation.

Dan couldn't help but notice his brother's anxious behaviour and sat forward on his chair.

"I don't know what to do. I'm losing my mind," Stephen stated, returning to his seat, putting his head in his hands.

"What's wrong? Is everything okay with the baby?" Dan asked, his initial thought was a complication with his sister-in-law's pregnancy.

"Everything is fine with Louise and the baby, but the fear of losing my whole family is what I'm worried about. I don't know how much more of this I can take or if I can even stop them," Stephen replied.

The response caused Dan to pause for a moment and swallow a hard lump in his throat.

"Them?" he asked Stephen, eyebrows scrunched, confusion pushing its way down his face.

"I know how this is going to sound, so please keep it between us for now, until I figure out what to do," Stephen said.

His brother placed his beer on the wooden floor beside him and clasped his hands, wondering what had Stephen on edge and then said, "Of course, you can tell me anything,"

"Okay, well, there is something out there in the fields. Like a fairy fort or something. I took the boys up there a while back to look around it, anyway I had to go in after their ball. Everything has changed since I did that, I saw them in there, I heard them on the way home that evening, and I've been seeing them ever since! I know they shouldn't exist but they do

Dan, they do!" Stephen continued, as he drank down another mouthful of ice-cold beer.

Dan sat speechless, waiting for his brother to explain further.

"You know my injured leg? Well it wasn't an animal that done it, it was the fairies who live out there in those fields,"

"Fairies?" Dan asked, ensuring he had heard his brother correctly.

"Yes, and now they want me to hand over a child to them or they said they will kill us all for disturbing them. Trust me, I know how this sounds but I don't know what I am going to do. They have already killed one of our neighbours," Stephen told his brother.

Dan took a moment to contemplate what he had just been told and as he looked towards his brother, noting the deep distress on his face and eyes growing heavier with each passing second, he knew Stephen wasn't joking. Various thoughts ran through Dan's mind about what could cause such a conversation and what could have influenced his brother to believe in such a thing, however he knew he had to hear him out.

"And you haven't told anyone else about this?"

"No, how could I? I know how it sounds and I know you're the only person who will believe me," Stephen said, as he looked towards his older sibling.

To Dan it all sounded unbelievable, he rationalised the move to the new house, being out of work for a while was weighing on him, and maybe his brother got a scare one night and was trying to connect all the dots as best he could. After all when it's dark, the mind can play crazy tricks on its owner. He could sincerely tell Stephen believed in every word he had said, so Dan decided to handle the situation as compassionately as possible.

"Okay, we will sort this out together, I promise you we will get to the bottom of this. I'm not going to let you face this alone, I'm here for you and going to help anyway I can," Dan confirmed.

These words brought with them a small fraction of relief to the pressure building in Stephen's head.

"Thank you. I knew I could count on you. You've no idea how good it feels to finally tell someone about them," Stephen said, exhaling deeply.

Dan was convinced it was all in his brother's head and believed what he needed was a little time out to help clear his mind of these awful and bombarding thoughts. He decided a day out was what was needed before it was time to call a doctor.

"I'm busy for the next couple of days, but I think we should hang out next week, just the two of us, so we can decide what to do about this. What do you think?" Dan proposed.

"You know what, I'd really like that. I just want to get things back to normal and to be rid of those creatures from around here once and for all," Stephen replied, thankful his brother was going to help him.

"Good, for now we'll keep this between us, don't worry I won't say anything to Katie," Dan said.

"Thank you," his brother replied as the door opened.

"You're both very serious looking, what are you talking about?" Louise asked, as she stepped into the room and picked up a picture off the mantelpiece to show Katie.

The men laughed in response as she returned to the kitchen to continue her conversation with her sister-in-law, which obviously involved or was related to the picture of her, Stephen and the two boys, taken three years previously, when they visited the west of Ireland. Stephen had been driving along the shoreline as the sun kissed the entire countryside and ricocheted off the still water, he decided to pull in at a car parking area to get a photograph of them all together.

For the remainder of the evening, Dan steered the conversation away from his brother's torment as much as possible to help ease the tension on him.

It was approximately 10:30pm when Katie and Dan decided to make the journey back to Dublin.

"Thanks for coming guys, I really enjoyed that," Louise said, as she hugged Katie and then Dan.

"We did too. I'm still stuffed after that dinner," Katie replied.

"See you next week, I'll call you okay?" Dan said to his brother, referring to the arrangement they had made together earlier that evening.

"Looking forward to it," he smiled in response,

relieved he had confided in someone and hopeful they would both find a solution to the creatures who were feeding off his fear.

"Look after yourself Louise, it won't be long until there is another little one running about the place," Dan smiled to her, and with that they walked to their car.

After their visitors left, Stephen checked around the house and called it an early night with his family. However, what he hadn't given much thought to was the warning he had received from the fairies about discussing or revealing their existence to others. What Stephen didn't know is, when he entered the fairy ring that evening and disturbed the creatures that lived within it, they hadn't left his side since. They lurked within the shadows unseen, monitoring his every move, relishing the pain and anguish they were subjecting him to. They knew he told his brother about them, and they weren't going to let his loose lips go unpunished.

"Maybe we could buy a place out here too eh?" Dan joked with his wife.

"Not a chance! I mean Stephen's place is beautiful but I don't think I could live so far from the city," Katie said, as she turned on the car radio to enjoy some music on their journey home.

Another thirty minutes passed by as Dan negotiated the narrow, winding back roads towards the city. It was quicker to use the country roads, as it would add a substantial amount of time to the trip if they had to firstly make their way to the motorway and then drive to Dublin. The road grew more narrow and steep in areas, however Dan alternated the car speed to account for the sudden level and width changes.

When the road opened to a safer width, and witnessing no oncoming traffic, Dan increased his speed again.

"Easy now," Katie smiled, noting the increase in acceleration.

"Don't worry, you're in good hands," Dan confirmed, as he shifted the car up a gear with a grin etched across his face.

A sudden splutter sounded from the engine which instantly caused Dan's mouth to widen whilst he rapidly scanned the dash before him for any warning lights.

"Everything okay?" Katie asked, feeling the car jerk around them.

"I'm not sure. We only had it serviced," her husband replied, still trying to decipher what was wrong.

A grinding noise filled their ears as Dan felt the engine's power leave the pedal his right foot was applying pressure to. Eyeing a space to pull the car in off the road a short distance away on the left-hand side, Dan allowed the car to roll safely to a stop on the gravel adjacent to the tarmac.

"That didn't sound too good," Katie stated, taking note of just how isolated they were with no lights twinkling in the distance through the heavy darkness.

"I know, stay here, I'll take a look," Dan said. He popped the bonnet and stepped out of the car into the cold night.

The smell of oil filled his nostrils as he fetched his phone out of his pocket, noting that he frustratingly had no signal. He switched on the phone's torch function and rounded the front of the car. Before he lifted the bonnet, he glanced to his right and noted they had in fact parked in front of an old, rusty field gate. He turned his attention back to the car and shone the light in his hand around the engine as best he could.

Nothing out of the ordinary could be seen, although the slight grinding noise could still be heard and from what he could tell, it was coming from beneath the car. He kneeled and directed the phone light underneath the car. He waited a moment and saw a drop of oil fall to a puddle on the ground below it.

Dan exhaled deeply and stood to his feet. He lowered the bonnet and returned to the driver's seat.

"Did you find anything?" Katie asked, while she wrapped herself in a thick jacket she had fetched from the backseat.

"I think it's the gearbox, a seal must have broken, and the oil is leaking from it. Do you have any signal out here?" he asked.

"No, I checked when you were outside, I've nothing, and my battery is nearly gone," Katie responded.

"I've none either," Dan informed his wife.

"What are we going to do? We are miles away from the nearest house and phone,"

"I know love, let's not panic okay? We will keep the engine running and wait here until daylight. Then we will go and get help," Dan stated as he turned up the heating, knowing the air wouldn't stay as warm when the car was immobile.

"Okay, but lock the doors and keep the lights on. It's creepy out here on our own," Katie said, moving closer to him.

"Don't worry I won't let anything happen to you," he grinned to his wife.

The countryside was silent and still around the couple stranded in their car as they moved themselves close to each other in order to share each other's body heat.

"Try to get some sleep. We'll set off at first light," Dan said, putting his arm around Katie.

Finding a comfortable spot to lay her temple against his shoulder, Katie stared out through the window at the car lights cutting their way partially beyond the ditch before them. After some time, her eyelids were about to seal themselves together, when suddenly she heard branches snapping, and rustling outside her door.

Katie jolted to attention and peeked outside, however, she couldn't distinguish anything due to her panicked reflection being present on the glass. She turned to Dan who was fast asleep beside her. Katie looked towards the digital clock on the dashboard, which read 03:53. Her attention shot back to the glass beside her upon hearing what sounded like footsteps move their way rapidly along the gravel outside her door.

"Dan," she whispered, an evident shakiness in her voice.

A light snore and a repositioning of himself on the seat, was the response.

Katie inhaled sharply, seeing something out of the corner of her eye, run through the lights projected from the front of the car.

"Wake up, there is something outside," she said, grabbing his arm and giving him a shake.

This was followed by a huge thump against the back of the car which quickly awoke Dan.

"What is going on?" he asked, as he turned to his petrified wife beside him.

"I don't know," Katie answered, checking the door was still locked securely beside her and glancing up to ensure the window was fully closed.

Dan held his breath, while his wife squeezed his hand tightly, as they both listened attentively for any further sounds from outside. The couple bravely stared out beyond the light projected from the car into the darkness to see if any movement within it could be detected. Dan reached into his pocket and retrieved his phone, looking at its screen, it still displayed no signal of any kind.

"Check yours," he whispered to his wife.

Katie did so and she saw that her battery had died.

Suddenly there was a loud thud against the driver's window, and out of nowhere sprung onto the bonnet of the car before them, the most hideous creature they had ever witnessed. The fairy stared through the glass at them as it donned its crooked, sharp toothed smile.

The couple sat paralysed with terror as the beast glared right into the very depths of their souls. The fiend moved closer to the glass, reached out its abnormally long arms, placed its claws flat against the cold windscreen, leaned forward and slowly ran its long, dark tongue from the bottom, towards the top of the window.

"What the hell is that?" Katie stuttered, as she forced herself as far back as possible into the seat supporting her, taking note of its long strands of black hair, pale white eyes, and pale skin.

"I have no idea," her husband responded.

Further advancement towards the car was heard outside. This was followed by Dan and Katie's attention being drawn to the door handles aside them moving slowly as something tried to open them from outside. They turned back towards the bonnet of the car, however their spectator was gone.

"What are we going to do?" Katie asked, as the panic rattled through her voice.

"Well we can't just sit here, they know we are here and can see us. I think we should try to hide out there, at least then they won't know exactly where we are and we will have various escape options," Dan said, referring to the large, dark field beside them.

"I think we should stay in the car, I mean I don't think they can get in," Katie responded, not relishing the thought of going outside.

"Whatever they are, they are just toying with us and if they break the glass we'll have nowhere to go!" Dan said, thinking of the story his brother had told him earlier about the fairies he had encountered close to his house.

Without any warning, the back window was smashed, causing the couple to jump in their seats.

"Okay, let's go," Katie screamed, rapidly changing her mind.

"On the count of three, we'll get out and run for that gate. If anything happens don't wait for me, stay hidden until daylight and go for help, okay?" Dan instructed his petrified wife.

With that he kissed her hand, let go, and slowly counted to three, breathing heavier after each number. The pair each, quickly unlocked and opened their doors, then sped towards the old, steel gate. Dan rounded the car at lightning speed and caught up on his wife. He helped her over the rough gate, as the stampede of feet closed in behind them.

Dan leaped the barrier as fast as possible, grabbed his wife's hand, and they both ran into the heavy darkness before them as the light produced by the car faded further and further into the background. After they had sprinted a great distance, their inhales growing heavier and heavier, Dan pulled on Katie's hand and they both quickly lay face down on the damp grass and held their breath as they heard the sounds of countless footsteps run just inches past them.

The pair remained silent for a number of minutes before Katie whispered, "Are they gone?"

"I don't know. We'll just stay here for now, I'm not taking any chances," Dan said, feeling his wife's hand trembling due to the fear she was experiencing and the extreme cold making its way up through her body.

She squeezed his hand even tighter, praying the creatures had given up searching for them, whilst she tried to concentrate on anything but the pain and discomfort the soggy, cold grass was causing her.

Dan raised his head and looked in the direction they had ran from, the lights from their car, now a tiny, distant glow. He looked to his right, however all he could see was a thick darkness beside them, the clouds in the night sky were doing a perfect job of drowning out the moonlight behind them. Dan looked back towards the car which left them stranded on the side of the road, he froze, eyeing a number of small figures scuttle from the left hand side of the field to the right, past the car light.

"Shush," Dan whispered.

Katie did exactly that, as she too had eyed the monstrous fairies scouting the area for them.

Looking towards the road they had been driving along carefree earlier that night, Katie prayed they would witness another set of car headlights, cut their way through the darkness so they could run for help, but would they even make it to the gate alive?

The night grew deafeningly silent and not a wisp of air moved around them, as Dan guessed to himself that a half an hour had passed. The pain and uncomfortableness from the ground, finally, became too much for Katie and she raised herself to her knees.

"What are you doing?" Dan whispered, as he kept a firm hold of her hand.

"I can't lay here any longer, I feel as though I'm going to get sick. We haven't heard them in a while, I think we should go. If we get to the road it would be easier to get help," Katie replied, as the drops of dew fell from her.

Dan thought about her rationale for a moment. The field had been the best option in the beginning to help them lose their attackers, however if they did make it to the road, they could create distance between them and the creatures, then wave a car down for help if one came along.

"Okay, but we need to be very quiet, we don't know where they are. Once we get back to the car, we are going to make our way back towards Stephen's place. There are some houses closer to us in that direction," Dan explained.

"Okay let's go," Katie said, feeling Dan raise

himself up to his feet beside her.

Katie quickly joined his side and the pair stood momentarily listening and watching for any sign of the creatures who had been hunting them.

"Come on, this way," Dan said to Katie, as he wrapped his arm around her shoulders and aided her towards their car, the engine of which was still running.

Following a number of steps, Dan glanced around them and fixed his eyes upon the lights in the distance once again, as the pair pushed their sapping feet through the long grass.

The sound of a branch snapping echoed through the cold, night air and the couple quickly shot to their tummies on the grass once again. Tears began to slowly run from Katie's eyes as she tried as best she could to contain the sounds of her crying beside her husband.

"Why are they doing this to us?" she whimpered.

"I don't know," he replied, equally upset, wondering what would happen if they were caught by the hideous creatures.

They waited face down in the grass for another couple of minutes and nothing further was heard.

"We're getting out of here," Dan said, as he stood to his feet, pulling Katie up with him.

Feeling eyes upon them but no movement, the pair quickened their pace, senses heightened, and marched towards their car as fast as possible.

Moments later, confusion crashed against the

couple as the gate they had earlier climbed to enter the field was nowhere to be found. The pair could see their car beyond the thick, undergrowth, the ditch of which had seemed to have grown even wider.

"It was here right?" Dan said to Katie, referring to the illusive entrance.

"Yes, it was right beside the car. What is going on?" Katie panicked.

"Come on, it has to be here somewhere," Dan said, walking to the left and then to the right, perplexed due to the inability to locate their exit point.

As he looked through the combination of heavy briars, branches and other foliage, Dan knew there was no chance of just climbing through it, their escape was blocked. Suddenly, the car lights before them died, and with it came inconceivable, raspy whispers from all directions. The beasts knew exactly where their prey was hiding. Dan's legs were grabbed unexpectedly and he was shoved to the ground.

"Run!" he roared to his wife, feeling the sharp claws dig their way deep into his flesh.

Unable to process the attack on her husband, Katie ran back into the blackness surrounding them.

"He should have never told you about us, it's his fault you're both going to die!" A voice snarled as the countless fairies which were holding him down, spun him over onto his back and latched onto his wrists and ankles to keep him firmly in position. The helpless man felt something climb upon his stomach and move up to his chest. Eyes adjusting, Dan looked deep into the pale eyes glaring back at him. Before he could open his mouth to plea for his life, the beast grabbed hold of the doomed man's neck and began to slowly squeeze.

Feeling the ice-cold claws constrict his throat, Dan thought of his wife and their son.

"One more of your filthy species erased and then we'll get her," the fairy said referring to Katie. "Blame your brother on this!"

"Please," spluttered from the defenceless man.

"Please?" The beast plunged its hand into Dan's mouth, wrapped its claw around his moist tongue, and with a firm motion, tore it from his body.

Mumblings of agony spouted from the injured man as he began to choke on his own blood. The fairy forced two claws deep into the man's eye sockets, popping them instantly as the unbearable agony increased.

"Just die!" the beast commanded, as it wrapped both its bloodied hands around his neck and crushed Dan's larynx.

Hearing her husband's struggle and then the sudden silence as she hid in the grass not far away, Katie knew the worst had occurred and she tried her hardest to contain her immense sorrow.

She ceased breathing as she heard numerous footsteps gather around her, accompanied by the sadistic whispering once more. Then silence, complete stillness, as Katie was left alone on the saturated ground to embrace grief, fear, and uncertainty of survival. She prayed heavily for daybreak so she could try to figure out a way to escape and seek help, however she wondered if that was even possible by that stage. Katie quickly began to rattle once again on the soft surface beneath her, however she was determined to remain in position until dawn.

An excruciating hour passed before the first sign of daylight began to trickle across the countryside. Katie looked about the area and saw she was alone. She quickly jumped to her feet, and raced to the general location she had fled from the monsters before her husband was brutally murdered.

She found the area to be empty, with no sign of his body. Katie quickly noticed the field entrance had returned to its former position. She didn't have any time to contemplate how it had mysteriously disappeared and then returned once day broke, until her attention was drawn to something laying on the road beyond the car.

Katie climbed the gate as quickly as possible, turned back towards the car and noticed it was a body lying on the middle on the road beside the car, her husband's body.

She raced over to him and instantly noted his, blood-soaked mouth, disfigured neck, empty eye sockets, and features of immense pain etched onto his pale, cold face.

"Please don't leave me," Katie cried, placing her

head against his motionless chest, as her tears saturated his jacket.

A sudden, ear shattering noise filled her ears and she quickly turned to witness a large lorry speeding towards her and her dead husband. The driver stomped on the brake petal as hard as possible and released the horn, gripping the steering wheel tightly in hopes the vehicle would come to a halt before smashing over them, however it didn't.

The front of the truck smashed into Katie's beautiful face so hard, her head instantly shattered into pieces, and her and Dan where rag dolled beneath the wheels. Blood splashed about the area, and the two bodies were crushed into unrecognisable pieces of raw meat.

The lorry struck the couple's car, which caused the front of the large vehicle to lift as its front wheel made its way along the body of the car, crumpling the frame as it did. The driver held on for dear life, as his truck reared up and flipped over onto the driver's side. The toss was so extreme, it violently flung the driver about in the seat, and when the cab crashed hard against the tarmac, his temple followed suit against the driver's door window, and cracked against the road, killing him instantly.

All that remained were two mangled and torn bodies, a crushed car, an overturned lorry with smoke beginning to hiss from the twisted engine and a dead driver inside.

Horror filled the next passer-by as she turned the

corner to witness the route obstructed in front of her. The elderly lady parked her tiny car safely and activated the hazard warning lights. She quickly unbuckled her seatbelt and made her way towards the scene of the accident, her main concern was to establish if anyone was hurt and if so, how badly.

She covered her mouth with her thin, veiny, wrinkled hand upon seeing Dan and Katie's bodies splattered across the road. She reached into her jacket pocket and retrieved her phone. She glanced to the signal indicator and quickly noted, like the two dead corpses on the tarmac before her, she too had no signal. She turned and went back to her car. With shaking hands, she negotiated the tiny vehicle into a U-turn and drove back in the direction in which she came.

After travelling back some distance, she pulled in once again safely on the road and checked her phone. A weak signal was present, so she quickly dialled the emergency services and informed them of the terrible accident she had happened upon.

When the Gardaí arrived, they sealed off the road and put traffic diversions in place to keep everyone away.

After the Gardaí rang the logistics company, the driver of the overturned truck was identified as a Wexford man who was travelling to work to collect his first delivery of the day. Dan and Katie were identified by a combination of what was found on their person and the paperwork found in the car.

The investigation concluded that due to the worn gears in the gearbox of the couple's car, the vehicle broke down and the pair stepped out in order to flag down the lorry, however he was unable to stop which resulted in the loss of three lives.

Numbness was the first feeling to crash over Stephen when the Gardaí called to his door the day they sealed off the scene and informed him his brother and sister-in-law had passed away in a tragic accident. He turned to Louise, hoping he was only experiencing a cruel, heart wrenching nightmare.

His first instinct was to jump into the car and speed towards the site where he had been informed Dan and Katie had met their end to prove that police had gotten it all wrong, and they were mistakenly identifying the bodies that had decorated the road with their insides. However, the Gardaí informed him he would have to go with them to the hospital to await the formal confirmation of the identity of the corpses.

As he walked towards the Garda car, Louise staying at home with the children, Stephen looked towards the fairy ring in the distance. As the distraught man took note of the heavy fog swaying around it, he was convinced they were behind the deaths.

Stephen went through the formalities at the hospital and waited for the confirmation to come through. Stephen asked to see his brother and Katie, however the doctors strongly advised against it due to the visual shock he would experience looking at what was left of their shredded and crushed bodies. They reminded him they were depending on dental records for formal identification.

When the confirmation came through some time later, Stephen plummeted further into the dark pit of emotional torment. As he sat in the chair with his face in his hands, he could visualise one of the creatures which dwelled in the fields beside his home smirking at his grief. Stephen was certain they were the cause of the deaths, but there was no way he could prove it, and the next thought was how was he going to break the news to his nephew.

After the funerals were arranged and took place, Brian, Dan and Katie's son, went to live with Katie's sister so he could try to rebuild his shattered existence, whilst Stephen returned home with even further strain and grief to manage.

Chapter 9

Alone in the sitting room, Stephen sat in early morning darkness staring blankly out the window. It had been a little over a week since they lowered his brother's cold body pieces into the damp ground, and Stephen was taking the loss extremely hard. Louise gave him time to himself on that Saturday morning, she brought the children into town to get breakfast and was going to bring them to the cinema later that afternoon.

Stephen hated himself for telling his brother about the issues he was experiencing. It was clear to him the deaths of Dan and Katie were a punishment due to him spilling his guts to his brother.

His attention was drawn to Mary's front lawn, as the darkness cleared, he noticed Claire standing, motionless, looking at him through the glass. Keeping his attention upon her, he watched as she raised her hand towards her statuelike face. He squinted further to ensure his eyes were not playing tricks on him, for in the girl's hand there appeared to be a large rat, squirming for its life. The girl looked towards the awe-struck man as she placed it before her mouth. She paused momentarily, grinned towards Stephen, and then proceeded to sink her teeth deep into the thick fur on the back of the rodent. The rat squealed in pain as she snapped its spine, and ripped a huge bite out of it, causing it to become limp.

Repulsed, Stephen ran to the front yard as the blood dropped from the girl's mouth.

"What are you doing?" Stephen shouted, running through the grass. "You'll get sick or worse!"

Reaching the girl, Mary's front door swung open, and he was quickly joined by the child's mother.

"Everything okay?" Mary asked, with a distant look within her eyes.

"She just... just bit into that rat," Stephen said, still in disbelief.

"Oh, did she now?" Mary said nonchalantly. "Claire go inside and clean yourself up!" she continued, without taking her eyes off Stephen.

"She'll need to get checked, she could catch a disease or something," Stephen exclaimed, baffled by Mary's lack of concern for what had just occurred.

"Oh, don't worry she'll be fine, children eh? Claire go inside, you know we cook them first," Mary laughed dismissively.

Stephen didn't see the funny side of what had just occurred.

"I'm sorry to hear about your brother and his wife. It must have been a terrible shock," Mary said.

"Thank you and it was. They had so much ahead of them, and I doubt Brian will ever get over losing his parents," Stephen replied to the creature, unknowingly to him who was disguising itself as his neighbour.

"Did they suffer?" Mary responded.

Stephen's eyebrows scrunched and pushed their way down his face with disapproval towards what he had just been asked.

"Excuse me?" Stephen snapped back in a venomous tone.

"I mean, did they die instantly, or did they feel anything? I often wonder that when people die and I know the circumstances surrounding their death. A little weird, but you have to admit, it crosses all our minds," Mary replied, a slight smile on her face.

The fiend in front of him was trying and succeeding in injecting further emotional pain into him.

"I'd rather not talk about this if you don't mind. I have to go!" Stephen said, turning away.

"Don't worry, we've all got to go sometime. Again, I'm sorry for your loss," the fairy replied.

The aggrieved man was unsure if he should reply with a thank you, or a get lost, however he decided to turn and walk away. He had more important things to worry about than the comments of his neighbour.

"I wish we could just kill him and the family, but I suppose we can't have all the fun," the fairy said to the other playing the role of its mother, when she returned to the house.

"He will break soon. Then we will watch as his world falls apart," the other creature, in the guise of Mary, replied.

Shutting the front door behind him, the thoughts

of his dead brother continued to plague his mind. Did he die in complete agony or was it instant? Did he call for help? Did he know he was about to die? Did he know how much he was loved? These were just a few of the questions which ricocheted around within Stephen's tormented head.

Not wasting any time, Stephen fetched the key to his work van, and threw on a jacket. He locked the front door, got into his van, and drove in the same direction Dan and Katie did on the night they were killed.

Stephen had not passed the scene since the accident had occurred, and while on route he wondered if he could find something which the Gardaí had overlooked to establish it may not have been a terrible accident, like he felt in his gut.

Stephen reached the scene of the deaths about forty minutes later and parked the car in the same location his brother had parked his own vehicle on that terrible night.

The first thing he noticed when he stepped out of the car was the deathly silence. Stephen knew the area was really isolated, so there would have been no source of help for quite a distance, and the time the couple had left his house that night, the odds of someone driving by would have been extremely slim.

The grieving man turned and looked back in the direction he had just driven from and noted the huge skid marks still evident on the tarmac. Stephen cursed the driver for killing his brother and wife, however looking at the scene and how close the corner was to the area the lorry struck the car, he realised if the lorry was travelling at a safe speed, as he was told after the investigation, it was impossible to stop the huge vehicle before smashing their bodies to pieces.

The road had been washed of body fluids after the area had been fully investigated, however he could only imagine the splatter radius. Stephen began to study the area to see if he could discover anything out of place. He scanned the road, the ditches on either side of it, and the area where his brother had parked his car. Nothing caught his attention as he slowly walked about the scene of the three deaths.

After scouring the site, he reached into his pocket and took out his phone. He activated the camera function on it, then snapped numerous pictures for further study later, because, although the road was quiet, it would look unusual if someone were to drive by and witness him searching about the area. Following a few short minutes and after documenting the scene, Stephen rested his arms upon the old, steel gate his brother and wife had been terrorised past.

As he stared into the large, empty field, he quizzed himself about what he was doing and what he expected to find. He thought himself stupid but at least he had finally brought himself round to visiting the place where they died. His thought process was obscured due to the pressure and fear of the fairies and the recent deaths he had to deal with. He knew he wouldn't be able to return to work anytime soon, as he couldn't focus his attention on anything other than the current items tormenting his mind. Stephen exhaled deeply and returned to his car.

As he journeyed back towards home, he wondered if there was anything he could do to keep the horrid creatures out of his house and a sudden thought sprung upon him. He would travel past the local church on his way back and deliberated if he splashed holy water about the house, would it keep the fairies at bay, creating a safe barrier so to speak. He could ask for the house to be blessed of course, however the priest may not be available to do it right away, and Stephen couldn't in his wildest dreams explain to the man of God why he was so desperate to get it done. He could spread the water around the house himself, and although he was not a regular church goer, he felt the act would deter the little beasts from entering his home.

After driving quite a while, the tall steeple with the cross proudly displayed upon it appeared in the distance, as the rain drops began to break against the windscreen. As he rounded the corner, Stephen saw the small number of cars scattered about the church carpark and as he expected, there was people praying inside, which meant access to the water font would be possible.

He parked the van near the two huge wooden doors which led into the building and switched off the engine. He searched the front door pocket beside him and retrieved a plastic bottle, the contents of which he had used to quench his thirst during a break on a job some time ago.

Wasting no time, Stephen opened the driver's door and briskly walked towards the large entrance to the holy building. As he stepped through the two wooden doors, to his right he was greeted by the holy water fountain with a crucifix displayed above it. He looked past the pews and noted the individuals near the front of the church praying. Their murmurs echoing through the building, he made his way to the water font.

As the desperate man filled the bottle in his hand, he stared at the crucifix before him.

"Please let this work," he whispered, eyes closed tightly.

Once full, he fitted the lid back onto the bottle, returned to his van and continued on his way home.

Stephen quickly parked the van in the driveway and then, bottle in hand, marched towards the front door. He couldn't get inside fast enough to begin spreading the holy water about the house.

Stephen unlocked the door, stepped inside, hung his coat on the hanger in the hallway, and unscrewed the lid on the bottle.

He placed his thumb over the bottle opening and began at the door. Releasing a trickle, he walked alongside all the internal walls within the house while silently praying, hoping with all his will this attempt at a holy force field would work.

Once finished, Stephen returned to the sitting

room and examined the pictures he had taken on his phone of the scene of Dan and Katie's deaths.

Swiping through the images, at first, Stephen noticed nothing out of the ordinary. However, after taking in a disturbing sight, his eyes widened and his jaw almost hit the floor.

Within the fifth photograph he had snapped, stood several pale skinned, jagged fanged creatures. Some had long, thick dark hair, others had only numerous strands sprouting from their scalp here and there, staring back him from behind the steel gate he had leaned against. He was completely shocked he had not eyed them when he was taking the photographs, and that they were able to follow him so far away from home.

He rapidly swiped his thumb across the screen to see if the fiends were in any other picture. Studying closely, Stephen saw they were not present in any other photograph. He scrolled back to the one which contained the multiple sadistic eyes staring at the lens, and swiped back through the four previous images. Stephen examined them like the others and didn't see any of the fairies in those either, they were only present in one picture.

Stephen returned to the image which had caused his distress and instantly his mind scattered once again due to emptiness in the photograph in front of him, his spectators had disappeared.

"No!" he roared, going through the images once more, trying to find the evidence he desperately needed to prove they existed. However, it was gone.

He slammed the phone against the table and threw his face into his hands. He was unsure how much more of the torment he could take before he finally snapped.

Stephen knew what he was experiencing shouldn't be real or indeed exist, but there was no denying what they were capable of doing and what they had already done. They had taken on the identity of Sean and continued to plague his life. It was at that moment Stephen thought of the incident with Claire earlier that morning when she bit into the disgusting rodent in her hands.

"Surely they haven't," he groaned. But then again, no child would be capable of such a thing, he thought.

He spun and glanced out the window to find Claire standing outside once more, however this time she was joined by her mother, as they both stared at Stephen through the glass. Looking at their motionless expressions, he was sure they too had to be shapeshifters, monitoring his movements.

He plucked up his phone once again and searched online for any further ideas he could use to keep his stalkers at bay.

Stephen found various sources of information, however the protection methods from the fairies varied with each site he visited. Some outlined that if you left specific items or herbs outside your house, or wore your cloths inside out, it could help deter the fairy folk.

At that point, Stephen was willing to try anything to protect his family, however he couldn't leave any of the listed items at the entrances to the building or wear his clothes inside out because his family would obviously notice the unusual behaviour. No, he was hopeful the holy water he had sprinkled around his home would prevent the unholy creatures from entering his house and terrorising his family in the future.

Louise and the boys returned home some time later, unaware of the actions of Stephen earlier that day. He had been working extremely hard to keep the existence of the evil creatures who dwelled near their house a secret from them.

"How are you love?" Louise said, giving him a huge kiss on the cheek.

"Good thanks, how was your morning?" he asked, as he turned to see his two beloved sons smiling faces, each holding a large bag.

"We had a lovely breakfast, went to the cinema, and we visited a toy shop," Louise said, smiling to her sons.

Both Owen and John raced to their father to show him what they had picked out for themselves.

"I'll get dinner started," Louise said, as she watched Stephen dig into the two huge bags with as much excitement as the children.

"Do you need a hand with anything?" he asked. Feeling somewhat relieved he may have prevented the creatures from entering his home ever again.

"No, no, you stay there. I'll call you when it is ready," Louise instructed as she closed over the sitting room door.

The family enjoyed a delicious meal later that evening and the boys returned to play with the new toys they had been treated to earlier.

"Oh, I just felt it move again," Louise said, rubbing her hand over her tummy. "I wonder if it's a girl?" she smiled to Stephen.

Stephen pulled her closer to him on the comfortable couch and placed his hand on his wife's stomach. Instantly, he felt a tiny thump against his palm, which filled him with immense joy, excitement, and pride.

"I love you so much, you know that," he said, before leaning over and giving her a long, slow, passionate kiss.

"Ewwwwwww," John said, before giggling alongside his brother, watching their parents engage in such a way in front of them.

"Hey, you two, less of that," Stephen said, quickly joining them on the floor and began to play with their toys.

The next thing that popped into his mind was work, and how he would need to get back to it soon to ensure his projects were going to plan and generate more money. Although the funds were still trickling in from his company, he wanted to take the reins again and he felt the sooner he did, the sooner he could begin to get his life back on track and concentrate on the most important thing to him, his family. He would do this once he was sure the house was safe from the evil invaders.

After the boys were tucked into bed later that night, the couple spent some time together watching television, as the fire crackled in front of them, the heat encompassing the pair in a warm, comforting blanket.

After some time, Stephen began to feel his eyes weighing upon him as he fought to stay awake. Sleep was certainly something which hadn't come easy over the last number of nights due to his wandering mind, so he welcomed his body's natural reaction to the tiredness.

Louise turned to him, seeing he was in a sound slumber, she reached for the remote and turned down the volume on the television. She laid her head against his chest and slowly drifted off to sleep alongside him.

Opening his eyes some time later, Stephen instantly turned to the clock on the mantelpiece, the fire below it had by then turned cold. Acknowledging it was after midnight, he gently woke his wife beside him.

"I was enjoying that," she said, rubbing her tired eyelids.

"Me too, let's go to bed its late," Stephen replied, directing her attention towards the old clock.

She agreed, rose to her feet, and enjoyed a long stretch accompanied with a yawn as Stephen placed the fire guard in front of the fireplace.

"You go on to bed, I'll lock up," Stephen said to Louise as he switched off the television.

"Thanks love," she said, as she placed a kiss softly upon his cheek and made her way to the bathroom.

Meanwhile, Stephen slowly opened the sitting room door, which led to the hallway to the front door and the boy's bedroom, to ensure he didn't disturb the sleeping children. He pushed downward on the cold front door handle and it didn't budge. Happy it was secure, he peaked into John and Owen's room to check on them. Their subtle breathing and still bodies beneath the blankets outlined they were both sound asleep. He checked the window in the spare room and returned to the sitting room.

"Don't be long, it's freezing tonight," Louise said, as she passed by him towards their bedroom.

"I'll be there in a minute," he smiled in response.

Stephen checked the backdoor, used the bathroom, then flicked off the lights, and joined his wife in bed.

As she laid her head on his chest, arm around him, Stephen once again felt safe in his own home following the ritual earlier with the holy water. In his mind, he could rest easy knowing those hideous creatures were now forced to stay outside, away from him and his family while they slept.

Relieved somewhat, it didn't take long for

drowsiness to overcome him once again and he happily fell asleep.

A couple of hours passed before he was awakened by what sounded like movement in the sitting room.

He held his breath, listening for any further noise, Stephen was still a little disorientated as he wondered if it had been a dream that had caused him to wake. However, there it was again! Footsteps moving around the room beside the one he was laying in.

He raised himself upright and looked towards his wife, the moonlight splashing against the curtains, helped him note she was still sound asleep.

Keeping as quiet as he could, Stephen pulled on his trousers, a t-shirt, and slowly made his way over to the old bedroom door, as the movements still sounded from beyond it.

Stephen instantly wondered if he had missed an area of the house during his form of blessing many hours before, however he had been, and still was sure he covered the entire building. He reached out and placed his hand on the cold doorknob. He glanced back towards his beautiful wife, knowing in his soul he would protect her and the boys until his dying breath, and slowly he opened the door.

Suddenly, the noises stopped as he peered out into the sitting room. Stephen couldn't see anything out of place as the shimmering moonlight bounced off every reflective item within the room. He paused a moment, certain he would see a tiny figure dart from one of the dark corners to another, however nothing!

Senses heightened, he gently pulled open the door and stepped out onto the cold wooden floor. Being sure to close the door behind him, he made his way to the opposite side of the room, while surveying the shadows for any sudden advancement towards him. His next concern was the boys, he had to make sure they were safe.

Stepping into the small hall and quietly pushing open their bedroom door, he breathed a sigh of relief when he saw the two boys were safe and unharmed. He pulled their door closed and kicked himself, thinking he had just done a night tour of the house for nothing.

As the night coldness started to eat its way through his skin, "Stephen," hissed a voice slowly from the kitchen.

A chill ran through his spine colder the air around him, as he bravely moved towards the source of the voice.

Slowly peering through the doorway, fists clenched, nothing could be seen or heard until his name was called once more from beyond the window in front of him. They were toying with him. Angered, he quickly flicked on the kitchen light.

He made his way to the back door and spun the key to unlock it. Fuelled by the need to protect his family, Stephen stepped, barefooted, out into the back yard.

It was a clear, crisp night as the bright moonlight illuminated the calm countryside and Stephen could not shake the feeling of countless eyes upon him. He took a number of steps forward, as the deafening silence became heavier around him, closing in on him with each passing second.

"Stephen," was spoken once again by a disembodied voice.

Every ounce of him wanted to turn and run back inside the house, however Stephen knew it would do no good and felt if he faced them this way, it would prevent them from going inside and harming anymore of the people he loved.

"Leave us alone, you hear me! I've had enough of this," he said, studying the general direction which he felt he was called from.

He carefully walked over to the edge of the yard which then became a garden and it was then they appeared to him.

"You're running out of time Stephen," numerous voices slowly whispered.

"I'm not going to do it. Leave my family alone, I was the one who disturbed you," Stephen replied, standing his ground in front of the fairies.

Suddenly, he was forced to his knees. The beasts closest to him stretched their long limbs out before them, gripped him with their sharp claws and held him firmly in position. Without warning, one of the creatures stepped forward, reached out its lengthy limb, pushed its hand into Stephen's mouth, and gripped his lower jaw tightly.

"You think you have a choice?" the beast said,

without moving its lips, pale eyes staring. "You think what you did with the holy water has any effect on us? We can come and go as we please but now we are getting bored. Give us one of your children willingly or we will take your whole family from you,"

"Please don't do this. I love them, please take me instead," the helpless man slurred, feeling the grip tighten further, as a rotten taste filled his mouth.

"Of course you want us to take you, but loosing someone you love dearly is far more painful to you and satisfying to us," the fairy replied.

The father of two, soon to be three raced for an answer and responded with. "Okay, I'll do it, but I need a little more time. I want to say goodbye in my own way before I hand him over," Stephen answered, as a tear began to trickle down his cheek.

"We won't wait forever! I could just rip this from your face and kill them all in an instant. Say your goodbyes and hand him over," the fairy said, as it moved its face closer to Stephen's. "If not handed over, we'll take everything from you."

The fiend released him and returned to the darkness alongside the others who had held him in place.

Stephen didn't jump to his feet immediately, he kneeled on the damp grass wondering how in the world he was going to get rid of the monsters tormenting him. His thoughts turned to his children and how would he ever in his wildest dreams decide which of the boys to hand over to the creatures so he and the rest of the family could live in peace.

He stood back to his feet and stared momentarily in the direction the little beasts had ventured off into and was greeted with total silence once more. Increased dread washed over Stephen as he glanced to the stars above, wondering why he was being subjected to such torment and what he had done in life to deserve such an ultimatum.

Feeling the damp clothing against his skin, he decided to go back inside before he became ill, a physical illness rather than the nauseating emotional stress he was being exposed to.

Stephen quickly relocked the back door and moved to his bedroom as quietly as possible. He changed his clothes and re-joined his wife in bed.

For much of the following day, Louise noticed an unusual silence about her husband. She put it down to the loss of his brother, however she could not have been more wrong. Of course Stephen mourned the death of his brother Dan, however the crippling emotional handcuffs that were restraining him were due to the unimaginable decision he was being forced to make.

Two days passed with little or no interaction between Stephen and Louise, over this time Stephen had been monitoring his children, absorbing how happy they were, and how much they loved each other and their parents. They had such a long life ahead of them and he had to decide which one to cut short.

Over the previous number of days Louise had been feeling a lot more movement from the baby growing inside her as the due date raced ever closer. She hadn't mentioned the growing cramps and exhaustion to her husband because he clearly had enough going on. Louise kept up with her check-ups during the pregnancy and all was going according to plan.

Of course Stephen offered to do more to help her around the house over the previous number of weeks, however Louise didn't want any fuss and with this pregnancy being her fourth, she prayed it would go smoothly like her previous successful two.

Louise's water finally broke the following Friday afternoon. Stephen instantly jumped into action. He phoned an ambulance immediately and made sure his wife was as comfortable as the situation would permit.

The morning started off bright and sunny, however the day had grown overcast and a light drizzle began to saturate the countryside. Stephen helped his wife time her breaths as she squeezed his hand each time the painful contractions began.

"Don't worry boys, Mammy will be okay," Stephen said, as they sat side by side in the sitting room. "John, can you go and get me a glass of water please?" he continued and turned back to his wife.

Following another twenty minutes, an ambulance sped to a halt outside the couple's driveway. Both paramedics quickly entered the house and instantly tended to Louise, leaving Stephen to comfort his children.

After examining Louise, she was removed from the house, placed onto the ambulance, and transported as fast as possible to the nearest maternity hospital.

Stephen followed the blue lights and squealing sirens with the boys. If life had of played out differently, he would have asked his brother and his sister-in-law to meet them at the hospital to take the boys for the night, but that wasn't possible now, that option had been taken from him.

When they reached the hospital, Louise was taken inside, examined once again, and then brought to the labour ward, the birth was imminent.

Stephen planned to be in the room during the birth, however, he couldn't leave the children on their own in a waiting room. Instead, he kissed his beautiful Louise on the forehead, told her how much he loved her, she made and was about to make him and the boys so proud bringing another member of the McKenna family into the world.

Sitting with his sons, Stephen had not cast any thought towards the beasts who lurked in the fields around his home. His only concern at that moment was his family, which was everything to him.

"Stay here okay, I'll be back in a minute," Stephen instructed John and Owen, as he stood to his feet and walked towards the toilet.

As Stephen stepped through the long, bland,

corridor, disinfectant filled his nostrils while he wondered how many people had ventured through the walls surrounding him, and how many new lives the building and its staff had helped deliver to the world.

He pushed open the door, used the facilities, and walked over to the sink to wash his hands. Doing so, he dried them, and looked at his reflection. Looking back at him was a visibly tired man, a man who was running on reserve, who had been both physically and mentally broken down, and was trying his best to hold everything together for the sake of his family.

His eyes flicked to the area behind him in the mirror and he quickly spun on his heels upon seeing one of those short, pale skinned, long haired, white eyed creatures grinning at him in the glass. When he turned, there was nothing there.

He placed both palms hard against his face. Even during a time where he should be full of excitement and joy, the things who lived in that fairy ring were on hand to remind him there was something for him to worry about. He turned back to the sink, spun on the cold tap, and dabbed his exhausted face with water. Raising his face, Stephen shot back from the glass upon witnessing his skin covered in bright red blood.

He swiftly reached for the paper towel dispenser and began wiping frantically, the body fluid smearing across his features as he did so. He threw the towel into the bin and reached for another when suddenly it was gone. No blood. Just the leftovers of some water once again upon his face.

He raced for the door and quickly closed it behind him. Taking a deep inhale, Stephen made his way back towards his children, stopping at the vending machine along the way, he bought two bars of chocolate and two drinks. He knew if there had been any kind of alcohol available, he would have bought some for himself to take the edge off.

When he returned to the waiting room, he found the boys sitting silently beside each other, staring at the white wall with various medical information posters displayed upon it.

Smiles graced their faces when the children eyed the treats their father had returned with for them.

Stephen sat down between them on the large couch and opened one of the wrappers on the bars and took a tiny bite out of it.

"Oh, you thought these were for you," he teased, which caused them to burst into a laughter.

After his brief mocking moment, Stephen gave John and Owen the chocolate and a drink each. No matter how hard he tried, he couldn't distract his thoughts away from the fairies and what they were forcing him to do. It should have been an immensely happy time in his life as he was about to welcome another addition to the family, unfortunately his mind was torn.

Another hour passed as Stephen looked at the time on his phone, time was dragging by painstakingly slow as he wondered how Louise and the birth was going.

Outside in the corridor, people were coming and going from various parts of the building and Stephen eyed one of the doctors stepping through the door.

"Well, how is everything?" Stephen asked, swaying slightly on tired legs.

"Everything is fine Mr. McKenna, both Mammy and baby are doing great. It was a smooth delivery, we are just carrying out some post-delivery checks and then you can go in to her." The grey haired, thin doctor informed the relieved father.

"Is it a boy or a girl doctor?" Stephen asked, unable to wait any longer to find out.

"Louise has just given birth to another, healthy baby boy," the doctor smiled, as he continued to complete and add information to a clipboard in front of him. "I'll come and get you once she and the baby are ready okay?"

"Thanks doctor," Stephen responded, and he returned to the seat, and placed his arms around Owen and John. "Did you hear that? You have a new baby brother," he said to the boys, as he pulled them close in a warm embrace.

He couldn't believe it, he was the father of another child, although he had been through so much, joy began to weave its way through him.

A half hour later, the doctor returned to the waiting room and asked Stephen and the boys to follow him into the ward.

Louise's warm smile was enough to help Stephen

cast all other thoughts aside. He released the boy's hands and they each sat on a chair beside her bed as Stephen gave her a gentle kiss on the forehead. He turned and witnessed one of the most beautiful sights in the world, the third time he had experienced it, a little human he helped create.

The baby was sound asleep, and its tiny gurgles and subtle breathing brought a huge smile to Stephen's face. Pride vibrated through his body as he watched his youngest son before him.

"Isn't he beautiful?" Louise said, as she held her hand out to her husband.

"He sure is," Stephen replied, taking her warm palm in his. "Come on over and meet your brother boys," he said to John and Owen.

The pair walked over to the opposite side of the bed and looked down on their tiny sibling. Both parents taking in the joyous scene before them.

"You will have to help me take care of him," Louise said to the children.

The couple had not decided on a name for their new child, although it had been discussed on numerous occasions. Due to everything else which had been going on, they had not reached an agreement, but they decided to have one by the time the baby was home.

The boys and Stephen sat with Louise until it was time to leave and allow her to get some much needed rest. Before leaving, Stephen gave her one more kiss and told her he would be back early the following morning once he ensured the boys were safely in school.

Once home, Stephen prepared dinner for the children, however he did not eat any of the meal himself.

Following some encouragement to clean their plates, Stephen instructed Owen and John to get ready for bed while he washed the dishes. He didn't want his wife to come home to a house where general chores needed to be tended to, because no matter how much he would try to convince Louise to keep her feet up and rest, she wouldn't be able to, knowing that things needed to be done.

He placed more coal onto the red embers within the fireplace and returned to the kitchen sink to finish off cleaning the pots and cutlery which had been used. Looking to the window in front of him, which was blanketed with condensation, he turned his eyes in the direction where the evil tormentors dwelled within the field he should have never set foot in. He wanted to enjoy the moment in his life he had helped introduce another child to the world, but his thoughts and worry would not allow it. Eyeing John and then Owen returning to the room in the dull reflection in front of him, Stephen turned and gave each of the boys a huge hug.

"Okay, goodnight. I'll be up to check on you in a bit once I finish up down here," Stephen said, and watched as they both walked through the sitting room of the old cottage, to their bedroom.

He stepped into the sitting room and turned down the television volume so the children could sleep easy. He then returned and finished what he had been doing.

Once complete, he peeped around the boy's bedroom door to ensure they were safe and sound, and he fetched a small glass and whiskey from one of the high cupboards in the kitchen. He flicked off the kitchen light and the one which illuminated the sitting room then lowered himself into the comfortable chair facing the large television. He poured a quantity of the liquid into the glass and took a sip, savouring the taste momentarily before swallowing, he placed the bottle on the floor beside him.

Stephen spent the next hour or so channel hopping, while trying to keep his mind on his wife and newborn child rather than those the fiends who wanted to break him down and ruin his life forever.

Surrendering to nothing interesting to watch on the television, he turned and daydreamed into the flickering crimson embers beside him in the fireplace. He had no idea how he was going to move forward after the initial joy of his new child and how his life was going to develop once the ultimate choice had to be made.

After finishing another glass of the strong beverage, Stephen's eyes began to bind themselves together and he eventually submitted to sleep.

Chapter 10

The alarm sounded on Stephen's phone early the following morning. He couldn't believe it when he awoke in the sitting room. He flicked off the alarm and glanced around his surroundings. A slight disorientation befell him as he raised himself from the comfortable chair which had been his bed for the night.

He went to his room, got a change of clothes, and made his way to the bathroom to get a shower before the boys got up for school.

He prepared a quick breakfast for Owen and John before calling them to get up.

Once he saw them off on the bus, noting that Claire was not outside to get it with them, he secured his house and made his way towards his wife in hospital.

During the journey, he pondered about his neighbour and her so-called daughter. Remembering the way he had reacted with the creatures recently, would Claire do anything to the boys while they were away from his protection in school? He rationalised they may be safe as long as he was making a decision in relation to which one of them he had to hand over to the fiends for undoubtedly endless torture. Stephen had so much weighing on him. His mind resembled a stretched elastic band which was beginning to tear at the sides.

Once he parked, Stephen stepped out into the soft drizzle and immediately pulled the collar of the jacket up around him.

Navigating his way through the long corridors, his spirits raised somewhat when he rounded a corner and stepped into the ward, greeted by his wife with a huge smile projected towards him. In her arms was their beautiful baby sound asleep.

"Hello love," Stephen said, as he leaned in kissing Louise, and gave his son a tiny rub on his cheek.

"Did the boys get up okay?" Louise asked, being the ever diligent mother.

"Of course, stop worrying. You need to concentrate on yourself for once okay?" he smiled, pulling a chair close to her bedside. "How are you doing, did you get much rest last night?"

"I did actually. This little one was actually very good," Louise said, raising herself up on the bed.

"Unlike the first two eh?" Stephen smirked.

Seconds later a nurse entered the room to check on the condition of the mother and baby.

"So, will they be able to come home soon?" Stephen asked.

"It's not for me to say I'm afraid," the nurse replied. "I will ask one of the doctors to come and see you both, but in the meantime, everything is fine here." She smiled before leaving to tend to other patients.

Louise handed Stephen his son. As with the first two boys, he was a little awkward holding the infant for fear of letting him fall, however the moment he looked down upon the new-born in his arms, immense love and pride filled him.

"I still can't believe we have no name," Stephen laughed.

"I know, what are we like?" his wife smiled to him.

The pair toyed with names back and forth before the doctor arrived. Following an examination, he informed the couple Louise and their newborn son could go home in two days.

Louise was overjoyed hearing the news, as too was Stephen until the thought they may be in imminent danger once they returned home crashed over him.

He stayed with Louise for the majority of the day before he had to leave to ensure he would be home in time for the children.

Even though he visited the hospital and stayed for a long as possible each day, when he left, it felt like an eternity to Stephen waiting for Louise and their newborn son to come home.

The couple finally achieved their goal of deciding a name for their son before he arrived home, they both agreed on calling him Michael.

While waiting for his wife and son to be released, Stephen had prepared the cot at the end of their bed. When Louise and Michael arrived home, she put him to rest in the cot which had held Owen and John when they were infants.

The rest of the family spent the remainder of the evening enjoying each other's company, Louise felt as though she had been away for weeks and was thankful to be home.

Slight coughs echoed on the baby monitor from their bedroom, "I better go check on him," Louise said, taking hold of the armrest beside her.

"No, you stay here, you need your rest. I'll go," Stephen quickly replied, taking hold of her hand, and directing her back onto the comfortable sofa in front of the fire.

Once he stood, the other two boys quickly took his former position beside Louise.

When he opened the bedroom door, the sitting room light cutting its way through the darkness inside, Stephen quickly shot back from it due to eyeing small, dark figures standing around the baby's cot.

"Everything okay?" Louise asked, turning to the startled man.

He turned to her, fear-stricken, and spun his head back towards the infant in the room. To his relief, the figures were gone.

"Fine… just nearly tripped over," was the quickest excuse Stephen could come up with.

"Well take your time," his wife smiled, before turning her attention back to the television.

Stephen walked over to his son, who was stirring in his sleep due to the pacifier falling from his mouth.

Stephen quickly retrieved it and placed it gently back into position in Michael's mouth. He paused momentarily, hoping his eyes had been playing tricks on him, and his sleeping son was safe from harm. Stephen checked the bedroom windows, both which were securely closed and returned to the sitting room.

Sitting back beside Louise, he kept glancing towards the screen on the baby monitor to ensure the child was on his own in the room. He wanted so much to confide in his beloved wife but he was sure she would think he was crazy, and there was no way he was going to put her through the torment when she was just home from the hospital. Stephen knew he had to stay strong for the sake of his family, and keep everything he had been experiencing under wraps to protect them from the same fate as Dan and Katie.

Sitting with his family, watching the two boys giggle at the television, he wondered how he was going to make the hardest decision of his life so the other family members would survive. How could he deal with the fallout, and would the sacrifice even make any difference? He cursed himself for ever stepping foot inside the fairy ring. The thought of moving away to a new house had crossed his mind more than once, however he was sure it would make no difference whatsoever.

Although he was extremely thankful he had welcomed another child into his life, he could not fully enjoy the experience and he could slowly feel the walls closing in around him, knowing the creatures would not wait much longer for him to make a decision.

Later that evening, he saw Louise off to bed and stayed up for another hour or so watching a movie before he decided to call it a night once the credits rolled on screen. Stephen checked the sitting room window to ensure it was locked, and then made his way to the kitchen.

Before flicking off the kitchen light, Stephen pulled one of the curtains in front of him aside, and it was at that exact moment he wished he had left it in its original position. Standing before him were countless fairies, they had swarmed around the entire house. One of the beasts raised its thin, wrinkled skinned hand and pointed a digit directly at the shattered, mentally torn man standing behind the glass. Seconds later, all the hideous faces which were glaring at him, simultaneously arched their pale, cracked lips, and projected an unsettling smile towards him.

Had the time come? He knew there was no getting away from the situation he found himself in, they could attack him whenever they wished, and it was clear they could freely enter and leave his home whenever they pleased.

Stephen released the curtain and walked towards the backdoor. He unlocked it and was positive he was going to be ripped to pieces once the latch disengaged, but he had no choice, he had to go outside and face the monsters.

He stepped outside and closed the door behind him. The beasts moved closer.

"I can't decide, please just take me," Stephen pleaded.

There was no reply, the fairies stood there, motionlessly staring at him as the coldness of the night seeped beneath his skin.

"I'll go with you right now. I go freely, just leave my family alone that's all I ask," the man said to the malicious audience before him.

Undecipherable whispers filled the air, however not one of the creature's lips moved.

"Please," Stephen added.

The whispering suddenly stopped. "We see you have added a new member to the family."

"Please just take me," the man pleaded, as the tears broke past the confinement of his eyes.

"You have twenty-four hours to make your decision or we will take them all from you," The creatures projected at him.

"But-"

Suddenly the light bulb in the kitchen smashed and darkness advanced instantly around him. Stephen was by then alone.

He stood paralysed in position. He had been given a definitive timeline and had absolutely no idea what he was going to do. Should he sacrifice one to save the rest or should he try his best to protect his family when the beasts came to take them away from him?

He turned and made his way back inside the house. He locked the door, even though he knew if they really wanted to, the things that preyed upon him could bypass it whenever they pleased.

Stephen, still numb from his most recent interaction with the fairies, cleaned up the broken glass, made his final checks in the house, used the bathroom, and went to his bedroom.

Stephen didn't turn on the bedroom light, as he didn't want to wake Michael, he would be due for his night feed soon and the more rest Louise and the child got, the better.

Stephen lowered himself onto the mattress beside his wife and stared into the darkness as his mind strained further and further. He had to make a choice, and no matter which one he decided upon, it was going to change his life forever.

Chapter 11

After several night feeds, Louise awoke the following morning beside Stephen, who hadn't closed his eyes during the entire night. He didn't notice her raising from the bed beside him. He glared at the cream coloured ceiling above him, wondering if he could bring himself to sacrifice one of the children to the fiends, and how would he ever explain what happened.

Stephen lay there as Louise got up to help the children get ready for school. Whilst the common, early morning activities occurred in the small cottage, Stephen numbingly remained in bed trying to decide what he would do as the invisible timer ticked away beside him until he no longer would have a choice.

"Stephen," Louise gently called from the bedroom door, "breakfast is ready,"

Even though she was just home from hospital, Louise wanted to get things back to normal around the house.

Stephen got dressed and walked down to the kitchen to find Louise had prepared a delicious breakfast for him, made up of sizzling selections of meat, fried eggs, mushrooms, toast, and a warm cup of tea.

"Morning love," She said, as she smiled towards

him.

He responded with a similar smile, only his was just for show.

Stephen lowered himself onto the chair in front of the food and glanced out through the window in front of his wife at the sink. It was a dull, damp day as the rain continued to gently patter against the glass.

"Owen and John are in their room getting their bags ready. Once they go to school I'm going to go to town and pick up a few things. I'll leave Michael here with you okay?" Louise said, turning to him.

Stephen still had not touched the food in front of him, his appetite was non-existent, however knowing he had her eyes upon him, he picked up the knife and fork, sliced into the succulent sausage, and placed the piece into his mouth so Louise would not question his mood.

"I can go if you like. You're meant to be still resting you know," Stephen offered, finally breaking his silence.

"Don't worry I won't break. I can handle a trip to the shop and back," she giggled.

Stephen paused. Looking deep into her bright blue eyes he never wanted to confide in her so much and explain the terrible situation he was in, however he couldn't do it to her. He saw the result after he had told his brother about the existence of the evil monsters and he did not want the same thing to happen to her.

"I know, but I don't want you to overdo it that's

all," Stephen replied.

Seconds later, the two boys joined them in the kitchen, while Michael slept peacefully in his cot in the sitting room. Louise instructed John to pull the door ajar after he stepped through it to help keep the infant in his peaceful slumber.

The family sat down and ate breakfast together. Once finished, Louise went to check on Michael. In the kitchen, Stephen looked towards John and then to Owen, "You both know how much I love you don't you?"

Both boys looked back to him smiling, while Stephen placed each hand across the table onto one of theirs.

"Keep an eye out for the bus. Don't go standing out in that weather," Louise said, pulling a warm coat around her shoulders and joined everyone at the table.

As the hands on the clock neared twenty past eight Louise instructed the boys to go into the sitting room and watch for the bus to stop outside the gate.

The bus arrived on time as usual and once Owen and John were safely on board, Louise kissed her husband on the cheek and left for town.

Meanwhile Stephen pulled the fire guard aside and cleaned out the ashes from the night before. He stepped out into the cold, stabbing rain, and fetched some firewood from the tiny shed adjacent to the small cottage. The broken man returned to the sitting room, lit the fire and sat across from it. Staring into the waltzing flames in front of him, he knew time was counting down closer and closer to the demise of his loved ones. Seconds later, Michael stirred in the cot which caused Stephen to snap out of his daydream, more like a nightmare.

He stood and walked over to the infant who had lost his pacifier and was beginning to express his discomfort.

Stephen quickly reached down and placed the pacifier back into position, and gently lifted Michael into his arms. He turned and slowly walked over to the sofa and sat down, while keeping his newborn son lovingly embraced against his chest.

The baby calmed and was once again enjoying a peaceful slumber. Listening to Michael's subtle breathing, a horrible idea entered Stephen's head.

What if I give them him? The very thought, making him feel nauseous.

He tried to distract himself by glancing to the fire and then out the window, whilst gently rubbing Michael's back. However, the thoughts continued.

He is so young, if I give him to them, he would never know any different and the rest of the family would be unharmed. It would be better than sacrificing one of the other boys because they would experience unimaginable terror, whereas Michael wouldn't know any different. Stephen couldn't believe these words were passing through his mind.

Michael yawned and moved his head slightly, getting a more comfortable position, before venturing into a deeper sleep in his father's arms.

Tears burst past Stephen's eyelids as he calculated giving up one son to save the rest of his family was an unimaginable answer, however he decided if he had to pick between the three of them, Michael was the best option.

He tightened his arms slightly around the infant as his heart shattered into a million pieces. Stephen wanted to scream at the top of his lungs, but he couldn't find the air to fuel the cries. He loved Michael so much and hated himself for ever bringing the wrath of the fairies upon his family. He decided that to save them, he would have to live with the eternal torment of handing over Michael to fiends in order stop the threat to his other loved ones.

Entire sensory numbness befell Stephen and he once again turned his attention to the dancing flames in front of him, eyes red, tears streaming down his cheeks, as his expressionless face came to the realisation of what he now had to do if he was to save the majority of his family.

He wondered how he would cover it up, but that would come later, all that mattered at that moment, was preventing four murders for the sake of sacrificing one child.

Stephen spent the next two hours with Michael sleeping soundly upon him, thinking over and over again if indeed it was the best decision he was making, and each time the answer came back, yes.

The fire had burnt to smouldering ashes when

Stephen heard the front door open, he quickly wiped his eyes before he watched Louise walk into the room.

"You two look comfortable. How has he been for you?" Louise asked, as she placed the shopping bags onto the floor.

No response came as Stephen gripped his son tightly, his mind still on the task at hand before him.

"Stephen?" Louise called.

"Oh sorry," he said, swinging his eyes toward her, "I was miles away there. Did you get everything okay?"

"Yes, and I'm back in one piece," she grinned. "Here, I'll take him for his feed," Louise continued, stretching out her arms for the infant.

Stephen didn't want to let the child go, he wanted to cherish every last second with him, however he didn't want to raise any suspicion. He handed the baby to his mother, stood to his feet, picked up the plastic bags off the floor, and followed Louise into the kitchen.

"I'll do that when I've finished here," Louise said to Stephen, as he began to find a place for the groceries.

Stephen didn't respond, he finished and returned to the sitting room. He had considered texting his foreman over the last number of days to see how the current project was going without him present, but there were more important things occupying his mind.

Louise entered the room a short time later to put Michael back to sleep. Stephen relit the fire and was sitting across from it once again. Louise laid the child down into the soft cot and returned to the kitchen to prepare for dinner.

Stephen didn't waste any time retrieving his son and once more sat down on the couch with Michael nestled comfortably in his arms. The heartbroken father fought hard to control the tears, cradling the son he was on the verge of losing forever.

Holding his beloved Michael, time seemed to slip by at an increased speed and he knew his window of affection was closing fast. Stephen decided he would wait until nightfall and when everyone was is bed, he would hand Michael over to the fairies to save the others. He would live with the consequences but would know he had made the only rational decision that seemed available to him. He stood to his feet, kissed the child on the forehead, and placed him gently back into the cot and joined his wife in the kitchen.

Stephen did his upmost to act normal for the rest of the day around Louise and for the remainder of the evening, once the two boys came home from school.

After the family had their dinner, they all retired to the sitting room to watch television and as Stephen stared at the clock, he willed the time to slow down but he knew it was pointless. After John and Owen went to bed, Louise also decided to call it an early night. She gently pushed the cot into the bedroom, then kissed Stephen goodnight. He followed by saying he would finish watching the program and join her.

It was creeping up to midnight when Stephen decided to lift himself off the soft, warm sofa on which he had been debating the act he was about to perform in his mind over the previous number of hours. He placed a jacket around him then went to check on John and Owen, seeing they were in a comfortable slumber, Stephen closed the door firmly once again.

He decided to leave the television on while he was delivering Michael to the fairies, thinking if Louise awoke while he was out, she would assume he was still watching his program.

Stephen pushed open his bedroom door and was greeted by two slow breathing patterns, both indicating that mother and child were asleep. He stepped quietly over to the cot, paused, looked in Louise's direction, took a deep inhale, reached down and gently collected Michael, careful not to wake him inside the house.

Stephen held the child to his chest as he left the room and shut the door behind him. Moving through the house towards the backdoor he prayed he would awake from the current nightmare he was experiencing. He slipped his feet into the Wellingtons beside the door, unlocked it, and moved outside. The coldness instantly picked at any available bare skin.

Michael stirred in his arms as he pulled the tiny blanket that was wrapped around him up over the child's head.

The father of three made his way to the front gate and turned right towards the entrance to the field he wished he had never set foot in.

Stephen held the child tightly in his arms as he climbed over the freezing steel gate and began making his way towards the fairy ring.

It was a calm night, following a damp day, and the moonlight was more than enough to guide him through the long, thick, saturated grass. With each step, Stephen knew they knew he had made his decision and they were waiting for him behind the thick fort boundary.

Michael became increasingly uncomfortable in his father's arms due to the cold temperature and the breeze pushing against them. The cold didn't bother Stephen however, the only feeling he had was immense grief.

Following a fifteen-minute walk, he reached the fairy ring. Tears poured from his eyes and he began breathing irregularly at the thought of what was about to come.

"Put him on the ground," whispered a shadowy voice from behind the dense undergrowth.

"If I do this, the rest of my family will be safe?" Stephen asked, holding Michael even tighter in his arms. Still unsure how he had reached the position he was in.

"Put… him… on… the ground,"

Stephen had no option but to do as he was

instructed. He hugged Michael tighter than he ever had before and kissed him on his cheek.

"I'm so sorry, please God forgive me," Stephen said, as his emotions got the better of him, and he began to sob loudly as he placed Michael on the blanket of damp grass.

The child began to cry as the sounds of snapping twigs and branches grew louder and louder. Moments later, Stephen was surrounded by countless fairies, their eyes fixed firmly upon him.

"We knew you would make the right choice," voices sounded from their unmoving lips.

"Please. I beg you. Just take me, you don't have to do this," Stephen pleaded. However, the words fell on uncaring ears.

One of the fairies stepped forward towards the distressed child, which triggered an auto reaction from Stephen to also move forward. This was short-lived however, due to the quick advancement of the other fairies around him, causing the distraught father to stop and witness the hideous claws wrap around his son.

"Please," Stephen said once more.

The beast smiled, teeth glinting in the moonlight, turned its back to him, and stepped back into the fairy ring. Stephen listened as the child's cries seemed to travel further and further away from him with each passing second until finally, they could no longer be heard.

Stephen was distraught and he couldn't do a thing

about it. Without warning, a bundle of rags were placed at the man's feet and from it burst a nauseating smell as a thick goo plopped onto the grass. Within seconds, lying on the ground before him was the imitation of a human baby.

"What is this?" the confused man asked.

"You will raise him as your own. We can't have babies disappearing without raising any questions, now can we? Your punishment is the loss of your child and raising another which isn't yours." With those words, the fairies began to retreat back into their domain.

Once alone, Stephen looked towards the ground at the monstrosity before him. He could not believe how much it resembled Michael.

He reluctantly picked up the creature and began to make his way home. The beast instantly began to cry a ghastly, inhuman wail as if mocking Stephen's torment and loss. The man's mind was overloaded with questions and what he should do next, however his main concern now was to get home before anyone missed him from the house.

"Shut up!" Stephen instructed the beast in his arms, as he stepped back into the kitchen.

A sadistic grin came in response.

He quickly, but quietly placed the imitation into Michael's cot and began to turn out all the lights around the house. When he returned to the bedroom, he could see the fairy child's eyes glaring towards him. He left the bedroom door ajar in an effort to not wake Louise. His head was thumbing with pressure and he felt as though it was going to explode at any moment.

Stephen got undressed, turned off the bedroom light, and climbed into bed beside his wife. The thought of locking the creature out of their room had crossed his mind, but he couldn't think of a way to explain the reason for doing so to Louise. Instead, he laid there listening to the evil abomination breathing at the foot of their bed.

Eventually Stephen surrendered to his tired mind and drifted off to sleep, and it wasn't until approximately five in the morning when he was awoken by an ice-cold liquid running down along his side.

"Louise?" he whispered, but got no response.

"Louise?" he called once more, while shaking her beside him, his hand now covered in something which was extremely cold.

Stephen spun quickly on the mattress and flicked on the bedside light. When he turned to face his wife, his life shattered into even more fragments witnessing the sight beside him.

Louise had been stabbed in the throat with a scissors she always kept on her bedside table. The scissors were still blade deep in her neck as Stephen checked for a pulse, knowing by the blank expression on her face, life had left her body. He pulled the scissors from the wound, and his mind quickly shot to the cot, leaping up on the mattress, he saw it was empty, and the door was swung wide open.

Springing from the bed, Stephen feared for the two boys and raced through the sitting room towards the hallway which lead to their bedroom. He flicked on the sitting room light and opened the door to find the fairy creature reaching up for the door handle leading to the boy's room.

Without hesitation, Stephen pounced onto the fairy and wrapped his hands tightly around its neck and squeezed as hard as possible.

"I did everything you asked, why did you kill her?" he roared.

The beast smiled at him.

"Answer me. Why?" Stephen screamed, forcing his hands tighter and tighter around the changeling's pale neck.

The only response was a widening smile before the creature, which was an exact replica of his son Michael, died on the floor.

"Daddy," a voice came from beyond the door which the fairy had tried to access.

Stephen fell to the floor realising now what had just unfolded.

It was true that indeed the fairies had just ruined his entire life, however the plan was to do more than they had revealed to him. Not only had be lost his newborn son, but his replacement had killed his wife and he had killed the evil replacement, which didn't put up any fight whatsoever. No. He had gone along with their malevolent scheme perfectly, because now it looked like Stephen killed Louise due to the fingerprints on the scissors and he had also killed their son.

Stephen knew the changeling had happily died to frame him and no one would believe him if he told the truth now. John and Owen would forever hate their father for what they would believe had occurred and he would rot in jail for something he didn't do.

As the boy's bedroom door opened and their screams filled the night air, Stephen cursed the day he set foot into the fairy ring beside their house. He couldn't live with the anguish anymore and the thought of Owen and John forever hating him. He turned to the boys and said, "I love you so much. Please believe me when I say it wasn't me. Stay out of those fields!"

He then dug the scissor's blade deep into his throat and ripped it from one side to the other. The pain from the laceration was nothing compared to the agony and heartbreak Stephen experienced as he watched his children rattle in terror, until his final breath.

The End.

About the Author

Chris lives in County Wicklow, Ireland. Folklore: The Second Tale is his fifth horror book. Chris is a huge horror fan and plans to write more stories long into the future.

www.chrisrushauthor.com

Other Books by Chris Rush

FOLKLORE
ALL SHALL SUFFER
THE LEGEND OF LOFTUS HALL
13 DEAD

Printed in Great Britain
by Amazon